Also by Nell Leyshon

BLACK DIRT

Nell Leyshon

DEVOTION

PICADOR

Thank you to Jonathan McGowan
Bournemouth Natural Science Society

First published 2008 by Picador
an imprint of Pan Macmillan Ltd
Pan Macmillan, 20 New Wharf Road, London N1 9RR
Basingstoke and Oxford
Associated companies throughout the world
www.panmacmillan.com

ISBN 978-0-330-42641-1

1 3 5 7 9 8 6 4 2

A CIP catalogue record for this book is available from
the British Library.

Typeset by SetSystems Ltd, SaffronWalden, Essex
Printed and bound in Great Britain by
Mackays of Chatham plc, Chatham, Kent

Visit **www.picador.com** to read more about all our books
and to buy them. You will also find features, author interviews and
news of any author events, and you can sign up for e-newsletters
so that you're always first to hear about our new releases.

DEVOTION

Tilly

Days are yellow and nights are black. That is because the sun moves in the sky. It goes up and down and side to side.

People live in houses and houses have roofs to stop the rain from coming in. They have beds in houses and they sleep in them. When they want to sit up they use pillows or get out of bed and sit on chairs which have legs, but the legs on chairs are a different shape from the legs on people. And sometimes people stand up and walk around. Or run. But a lot of the time they sit. And they lie down to sleep all night. They take their clothes off to sleep. I think you can sleep if you keep them on, it's just you're not allowed to.

People keep animals in their houses. They keep them in cages or tanks unless they are cats or dogs. They like mice if they are in cages but if they are running round they have to kill them as the mice eat all their food and it would make them hungry. They take dogs for walks on leads but cats go for walks on their own. I don't think mice go for walks.

My dad has insects in tanks and he looks at them a lot.

If one of his insects loses a leg a new one grows back. But the new one is usually green. Even if the insect is brown the new leg is green. I don't know why.

These are things I know. A thing you know is some thing in your head. It is inside there, just behind your eyes. I have lots of things inside my head. This means I can think. Thinking is saying things but there is no sound. You can decide to say a thing out loud if you like, and it can still be in your head even if you have said it. If you don't say it and keep it inside your head then it becomes a secret.

I didn't wake my sister up.

Sometimes my sister tells me stories. A story is in a book and things happen in it. I have a book all about an insect who is unhappy. It is a praying mantis, like my dad keeps.

I eat apples and they make a sound inside your head when you eat them.

Moss grows on stones and there are green circles called lichens. They don't move but it's not because they are lazy. It's because they don't have legs. So they couldn't have a green leg at all, even if something fell off them.

Moss is soft and sometimes the birds pick it up in their beaks and fly away with it. They take it to nests and stuff the moss in so their babies have beds to sleep in.

Babies like to lie in something soft. That is because they can't stand up because their legs are soft.

★

I didn't wake my sister up, even though I wanted to.

I walked past her room, but the door was shut, so I walk-ed past and went down the stairs into the kitchen. She gets cross if I wake her up, even if I have something really import-ant to tell her.

She smells nice, my sister. Sometimes she lets me get in her bed and I can get the smell on me. I like it when that happens.

Yes, I like it.

So I didn't wake her up. I didn't know what to do so I went into the kitchen. I found an apple which was red but it had some yellow and green on it and the skin had tiny brown dots like freckles on.

I rubbed the skin of it on my leg and looked at it, but there was no shine. I did it again and again, but there was still no shine. Stupid apple. I squeezed it hard and dug my nail in it.

It was my dad who told me about the insect leg growing back green. He might have got his colours wrong. But I don't think so. He knows all different things about different things. And he doesn't get things wrong. Sometimes when he tells me things he says we'd better check and he gets a book out and shows me how to check a fact. He's always right. Always.

His books are still here even though Dad isn't.

I watched him drive off with his car full of insects and suitcases and boxes, but I don't know where he went.

Grace

My sister Tilly sat on the kitchen table, wearing her pants and nothing else. Her dark hair was messy from the night's sleep and her skin was tanned from playing outside. Her book was open on the table and she held an apple in her hand. She looked at me as I walked in.

—You okay? I asked.

She said nothing and started rubbing the apple along her bare leg. I walked to the kettle and filled it, then flicked the switch.

—You won't get it to shine like that, I said. —It doesn't work on skin.

She shrugged and continued rubbing. I looked over towards the back door and saw a jacket hanging there. Dad's jacket, his blue lightweight one for walking. He must have forgotten it. I went over and took it off the hook, folded it and held it. Tilly watched me and our eyes met and we knew.

This was it now, the three of us.

I put the jacket down and went to Tilly. I reached my arms out to her, but she pulled her legs up under her chin and held herself instead, shaking her head, her hair moving, brushing her knees.

—Come here, I said.

She shook her head.

—Come on, I said. —Come on, Til. You'll see him soon.

I waited for her to speak, but she didn't, so I walked over to the kettle and made the tea. I put Tilly's by her on the table and took Mum's up to her. I went up the first flight of stairs, then up again, to the top floor.

Her bedroom door was closed, and I turned the handle, then pushed the door open with my shoulder.

Light came through the red curtains, staining the room pink. I stepped over a pair of jeans on the floor and it was then I saw him. A second head on the pillow.

My mother lay asleep, her back to me. Her arm across a man. His face was turned away, but I could see dark, closely cropped hair. His shoulders were pale and pockmarked. There was a tattoo on the base of his neck, thick black ink in the shape of a wave. And around his upper arm there were letters, spelling out a name. DAVE.

My mother's dyed red hair was spread over the pillow. Her skin was tanned and she wore her silver bangles on her arm which was draped over him. Her arm, over him. This person I had never seen before.

I put the tea down by the bed and took a step backwards. My bare feet touched his jeans on the floor, his pants tucked into them. Blue cotton, inside out, the gusset of them like a secret underbelly.

I ran out of the room, down the stairs, back to the kitchen. I picked up my mug and held it tight to stop the shaking in my hands.

Tilly looked at me. —There's a man in Mum's bed, she said. —What's he doing there?

I said nothing. Just held my tea tighter, though the china felt as though it was burning my hand.

—Gracie, she said. —What's he doing there?

I opened my hands and the mug fell. It smashed and tea spread across the tiles, wetting my feet. We stayed there, me looking at the floor, Tilly looking at me. Then after a while I said, —You better get dressed. You're gonna be late.

She slipped off the far side of the table and ran out of the room.

I stood there for a while until I heard footsteps on the stairs. I wanted to move, run away like Tilly, but it was too late. I saw her feet enter the room, chipped blue varnish on her toenails, silver ring on her second toe. And the bottom of her dressing gown, red satin with the tail of a black dragon.

We both stood in silence, my eyes looking down at the broken china. Leaking into the tea there was a small fern-shaped spray of blood from my foot.

I watched her move across the room and heard her open the drawer where we kept the towels. She came closer and bent down to mop up some of the liquid, gathering the pieces of china. I moved my foot and she knelt back on her heels.

—You've hurt your foot, she said.

I said nothing.

—Grace.

—It doesn't hurt, I said. I lifted it on to the chair and wrapped a tissue round it; the thin white paper absorbed the blood. Mum watched.

—Is it okay?

—It's fine, I said.

She took a newspaper from the pile and put the broken china in it. I went to go to my room.

—Grace, she said. —Where's Tilly?

—She's gone to change.

—Grace. She made my name sound ominous, and I knew she had more to say. Please, I thought, please don't say anything. Please allow me to go.

But she continued. —Look, Grace, she said. —He's just a friend.

I looked out of the window, at the red and blue climbing frame and the apple tree beyond. If I said nothing, maybe she'd stop talking and let me leave.

—He is just a friend. Okay?

I took a step towards the door and the stairs and my room. —I've got to get dressed, I said. —I'll be late.

—Have you had breakfast?

I shook my head. —I'm not hungry.

—I'll make you both something.

—I don't want anything.

I left the room and ran upstairs and as I ran I thought, she's never made us breakfast. Dad does that.

★

I sat on the side of my bed for a while and waited for my hands to stop shaking.

When I calmed down I dressed for school, then looked at myself in the mirror. My long dark hair was scraped back from my face, which was pale, even in summer. I'd inherited his skin, not the dark, oily skin that she'd passed on to Tilly.

Then I thought of *his* skin – white, pockmarked, tattooed. I shook my head as though I could get rid of the memory. I grabbed my school bag and ran downstairs. I was going to go straight out of the front door without saying anything, but Mum was blocking the way, Tilly with her, book in one hand, lunch box in the other.

—Grace, Mum said.

I refused to look at her.

—I made you some breakfast, she said.

—I told you. I'm not hungry.

—You haven't got any money.

She went into the kitchen and I heard her shake some coins out of the jar. I stared at the tulips on the hall table. They were dying, their yellowing stems drooping down in long curves, the red petals falling on to the floor.

She reappeared and gave me the money. —Here, she said, —have some extra.

I opened the front door.

—And don't forget, your dad's picking you up.

I stopped for one second.

—Did you hear me? I said your dad's picking you up.

I turned back to her. —Is he?

—He is, yes. Look, Grace, will you stop being like this.

—Like what? I asked.

—You know what. For God's sake, I told you. He's just a friend.

—I'm sure he is, I said. I took Tilly's arm. —Let's go.

We stopped at the school gate, and I brushed Tilly's hair out of her eyes, ran my fingers through it and straightened her collar. —Wait here for Dad this afternoon, I said. — Okay?

—Why's he coming?

—Because he is.

—Grace. I waited, but she said nothing else, just stood there with her mouth open.

I rubbed her arm. —You'll want to see him, won't you?

She nodded. —Grace, she said. —Will you read me my story?

—I can't. You have to go in or you'll be late.

She held the book out. —Please.

I shook my head. —I read it to you last night. You know every word of it.

She pushed the book into my hands. The cover, made like the rest of the book by Dad, was the triangular head of a praying mantis, her eyes staring out and her front legs clasped together. The title above the head: *The Unhappy Insect*.

—Please, Gracie. Just read the first page.

—Just that, then you have to go. You promise?

—I promise.

I took the book. The spine was cracked and worn, the inside pages torn. I opened it and found the first page. I bent down so Tilly could see, and I started to read.

The Unhappy Insect

Manty the praying mantis lived in a glass tank in a room in a house.

The tank was nice and big and had lovely clean earth on the floor and green leaves. Manty spent her days learning to eat crickets and flies.

One day the lid of her tank opened and a big hand came in and lifted Manty out. She was put in a cardboard box and taken away.

Manty had to push her legs against the sides of the box to stop herself falling over. She could hear voices. Human voices. After a long time everything stopped.

The box was opened and the light streamed in. The box was suddenly tipped up and she slid into her new home.

Grace

When I had finished, Tilly closed the book and tucked it under her arm. She gave me a quick hug and ran across the playground. Before going into her classroom she turned and waved.

I looked up the hill towards my school and tried to imagine myself there at my desk, but I couldn't. Instead I saw her arm on his white skin. The ink of the tattoo and the black letters. His pants curled up in his jeans.

I took my phone and put it in the bin, then started walking down the hill. I walked along the High Street, past the last houses, and over the river, where the fields began.

I didn't know where I was walking or why. All I knew was I wanted to keep going, away from home.

I walked through the fields until I reached the woods bordered by the old railway. The path was flat and green and shaded by overhanging trees, and I walked along it briskly, as though if I were quick enough, I could leave my thoughts behind.

It was a warm day, nearly the start of the summer holidays, and I followed the same path we'd taken the year before. It had been the three of us. Dad had asked Mum to come, but she said no, she had things to do.

As always when he took us walking, he'd packed a box of sandwiches in his rucksack, with bottles of water and apples. His map was in the plastic cover and hung from his neck on a cord. We stopped under a tree and Dad sat on a stone and handed the food around. The sun was warm then as well, and after we'd eaten, Dad showed Tilly tiny scraps of lichen on the stones and branches. I watched him in his shorts with his thin legs and blond hairs, his sharp knees. Tilly wore a denim skirt that showed her fat legs, the pleats at the back of her knees, and I felt a flash of irritation with them. The thin, stretched tendons of his legs, the shapelessness of hers. The endless patience of him, showing, teaching. That moment was the first time I felt the three of us became the two of them, and I became the observer, sitting watching from a distance.

I moved my school bag, took the weight on to the other shoulder. I wondered why this one memory had returned to me now, and what the point of it might be. But before I could work it out, I saw a dog standing in the long grass to the side of the path. I looked around for its owner but couldn't see anyone. The dog barked. I still couldn't see anyone. Then it walked towards me. I held out my hand until it came close enough to smell me. It rolled over and I saw it was a girl, saw her white belly with its brown spots. I felt for her leather collar, but there was no tag.

The dog jumped to her feet and barked again.

—What is it? I asked.

She barked yet again, then walked away from me and stopped, looking back. There was still no sign of her owner. I called aloud, but no one answered. She repeated her action – barking and moving off, then stopping and looking back.

—What? I said. —You want me to follow you?

I followed her and she led me to a gate. She wriggled beneath and waited while I climbed over it, before running ahead again, into the wood.

The sun came through the leaves and dappled the ground. The grass was shorter here and the path caked dry. Dead branches broke easily under my feet, the wood rotted and fragile. There were a few brambles, and one caught my leg, the thorn digging into my ankle. The dog waited, panting, watching me.

—I'm not coming, I said.

The dog stared, her head tipped to the side.

I went to turn back, but she barked. I shook my head. She barked again, louder this time, and I took a few steps forward. —*All right*, I said, although my bag was heavy and the cut on my foot was hurting.

Round the bend of the path there was a large tree with a circle of bare earth beneath, dead leaves scattered around. The dog started whining and I was aware of something red in the leaves. She ran to it and lay there, and I followed cautiously, not wanting to get closer, not wanting to see. But of course I already knew what it was, even before I'd really seen it.

My mind made it out in separate pieces. A red shirt. A pair of denim-clad legs. Leather boots. Then the pieces joined together and I saw a man, with too-pale skin and pale hair, lying in the dark leaves.

I wanted to run back along the path, back to the railway line, but I forced myself closer and made myself kneel by him. He was older than me, around twenty. His eyes were closed, and I didn't know whether to speak, or shake him, or try to move him. I reached out and brushed a leaf off his cheek, and as my finger touched his skin, his eyes opened.

His eyes were a grey-blue and one appeared brighter than the other; then I realized it was because one pupil was larger. It seemed as though he was having problems focusing on my face, as though he was seeing something beyond me.

The dog moved as if to lick his face. I pushed her away.

I spoke quietly. —Are you all right?

The dog nosed forward again and I pressed down on her haunches, got her to sit, her tail brushing through the dry leaves.

—What happened? I asked. He didn't answer.

I looked up and saw the spreading branches above, a rope knotted over one of them, the end of it frayed, swinging free. Then I saw the raw, red marks on his neck.g

—I'll go and get some help, I said.

He tried to lift his head, and I put my hand out.

—Try not to move. I'll be as quick as I can.

He closed his eyes, then opened them again. —What's your name?

—Grace, I said.

—Who sent you? Someone sent you here.

—I have to go and get help, I said.

—No, he said. —Don't go. Don't leave me.

—I have to.

I patted my leg to call the dog and we ran together towards the main road.

Andrew

I had driven right through the night, following the path of the river. I drove from where I now lived by the sea, into the countryside and through the dark town. Then I turned and retraced my route, all the way to the sea again. Sea to the town, town to the sea.

As I drove I listened to a Bach fugue and after a while there was a synchronicity between the movement of the music and the passing road signs and occasional oncoming headlights. This must have allowed me to slip into my own temporary fugue state, for I was suddenly aware of the tyres hitting the edge of the verge. It was time I went back before I had an accident.

The sky was starting to change as I drove through the town and over the bridge that crossed the river, through lanes and fields to the sprawled and extended village where the river flowed out to sea.

The house was at the far end of the village, in a quiet, unlit road that ran parallel to the water's edge. It was the last of a terrace of what had once been identical houses but now had doors and windows of different designs and colours: two had cars parked in their old front gardens; one had a large boat covered in a blue tarpaulin.

I pulled up outside, turned off the engine and sat there for a while. I finally felt tired, and as I let myself in and climbed the stairs to my room, I thought I might even manage to sleep for a few hours; however, as soon as I was in bed, every trace of tiredness left me, and my mind was alert again.

I propped up my pillows against the green velvet head-board, and lay back. My bedside lamp was not yet unpacked, so the room was illuminated by the large brass light fitting hanging from the ceiling. Two bulbs were functioning, one missing. On the wall opposite the door, at the end of a stretch of green carpet, there was a fake fireplace designed to replicate the original, which would have been ripped out years before. The wooden mantelpiece was painted in thick cream gloss, and the inner panels appeared to be marble but were, I imagine, reconstituted and polished cement. The entire house had been refurbished so the inside appeared brand-new; only the outside made it clear it had stood for many years, housing families who had survived by working on the water. Before moving in, I had visited on numerous occasions, but never really explored the area, and I planned to take this opportunity to do so. I had bought myself a large-scale map, and studied the public pathways and the course of the river; I'd also found a second-hand book on the history of the waterway and intended to follow the river, right from the mouth, where it spilled out from the mudbank tonsils into the sea, back up its path through the town, eventually arriving at its source.

I looked at my clock: it would soon be time to get up, although I had not yet slept. Perhaps this was the day to start exploring; I'd need a large breakfast first, to keep up my energy levels.

It was the thought of breakfast that began to unravel my intentions. I suppose it was the realization that when the sun had finally fully risen, I would not have my daughters with me, would not be back in the familiarity of our home, but here still, among my unpacked possessions.

To stop myself dwelling on the girls, I crossed the room and opened the box of books I had brought. I took out the padded envelope and opened it. The book was still sealed in a plastic bag and I carefully peeled off the sellotape and slid it free. It smelled musty and the edges of the pages had yellowed but, as promised, it did not look too worn. The cover was a faded blue cloth, the dust jacket long missing. The title was in distinctive, old-fashioned gold: *Mantids and Other Dictyoptera.* I leafed through it at random and lifted the sheet of thin protective tissue to look at a photograph. It was difficult to judge the accuracy of the reproduction, as one has to account for the effects of time and any exposure to light on the print, as well as the reliability of the levels of colour, but it seemed of a good quality, considering the date of publication. A mantid with brown wings unfolded. *Deroplatys desiccata. Known to mimic dead leaves.* I closed the book, and placed it on the bedside table.

I stepped over the extension leads and picked up the water sprayer from the trolley. The tanks stood on large metal shelves, the glass walls streaked with moisture and the floor covered in damp vermiculite; I lifted the first lid and sprayed a fine mist into the atmosphere. The mantid in the next tank hung from a large privet twig and I could see the beginning of a split on her back. I watched for a long time, transfixed, as the split widened. She twisted to free herself, and I could see the paler, fresh flesh beneath. Her new body wet and flexible, she slowly reversed out, until she was free of the old skin which fell to the floor of the tank. She clung to the twig, waiting for her new skin to darken and harden.

It was not the first time I had seen this, but my act of witness in the dawn of that particular night felt as though it should bring me hope and signal some portent.

I reached into the tank and took out the skin she'd shed, and laid it on the palm of my hand. It was virtually weightless, and I examined it carefully under the light before depositing it on the table and getting into the bed. I picked up my new book again and stroked its cover and opened it. I read a few paragraphs.

Mantids and Other Dictyoptera

The two main groups of insects in the order of Dictyoptera (Greek: *dictyon* = net; *pteron* = wing) are mantids and cockroaches. It should be noted that in some taxonomic schemes they are listed as two separate orders.

In both mantids and cockroaches, the sexual parts are hidden underneath the abdomen; females have six abdominal sections and males have eight. The mantids deposit their eggs in a papery case, the *ootheacae*, which is fixed to a twig or other surface. Metamorphosis is incomplete: there is no maggot or caterpillar, but a series of wingless nymphal stages, which resemble adults.

The suborder Mantodea is divided into eight families: Chaeteesidae, Metallycidae and Mantoididae (all three each containing one small genus); Amorphoscelidae, Eremiaphilidae, Hymenopodidae and Empusidae; Mantidae, which contains the majority of the species. The exact number of mantid species remains in dispute, but is in excess of 2000, and they are to be found in temperate or tropical climates.

The mantid has the *hypognathous*, the inverted triangular head, and both simple and compound eyes. The simple eyes are three ocelli, also in a triangular pattern and situated between the antennae. The two compound eyes have up to 10,000 ommatidia each.

The mantid has two raptorial front legs which have been developed to seize prey, the femur and tibia having rows of sharp spines.

The front legs are clasped together as though in 'prayer', and the mantid combines a highly developed method of attack with extra-ordinary patience and camouflage skills, making it a ruthless and brilliant survivor.

Andrew

When I heard the car pull up outside, I closed the book and placed it back on the table.

I listened as the engine was turned off and the car door opened then slammed shut. There was the electronic beep of the locking mechanism, then the key in the front door of the house. I heard the clunk of the door closing and the dead weight of the black leather bag as it dropped on to the floor in the hall.

I turned and lay on my side for a while, before getting up. Taking some notes from my wallet, I went downstairs.

Barbara stood by the kettle; one of her feet was flat on the floor, the other was tucked behind her leg. She brushed her short, light blonde hair away from her face, then rubbed her eyes and yawned. She opened the cupboard door and took out a mug.

I cleared my throat. She jumped, and turned towards me, her hand resting on her chest as if to still her heart.

"Christ," she said. "You scared me."

I cleared my throat again. "Sorry. I didn't mean to. I

heard you coming back. I mean, not that you made an unnecessary noise. I was awake anyway. How was the night shift?"

"Good. Tiring."

I slipped my hand into my pocket and took out the folded notes. "Here."

After a second Barbara took them and put them by the kettle.

"It's the rent money," I said.

"I guessed that." She smiled. "I'm making tea. Would you like some?"

"I don't want to put you out."

"Does it look like it'll put me out? I said I'm making it."

"Then yes. Thank you."

I walked to the glass doors which led into the garden. There was a small lawn with a table and chairs, and beyond the scrubby hedge at the bottom there was the common land that ran down to the river bank. To the right I could see the metal structure of the old dock, where there were a few ruined boats which twice daily got stranded on the mud flats at low tide.

"Did you sleep all right?" she asked.

"I'm not sure I'd call it sleep," I said. "It always takes me a while to drop off somewhere new. Some primitive instinct, I imagine, keeping me from harm."

Barbara took a couple of tea bags from the tin. "Do you think?"

"In terms of world history," I said, "sleeping in a cave was not that long ago."

She smiled again. "I suppose not. So what do you do when you can't sleep?"

"Last night I went for a drive."

"Where?"

"I don't know. I drove automatically. It was something to do. I didn't want to lie in bed, wide awake."

I heard the fridge door open and close, then the lid of the metal bin.

"Andrew?" She held the mug out. I took it, put it on the table. She scrutinized me closely. "Are you all right?"

"I'm fine," I said. "Absolutely fine."

"You're okay here? I mean, you like it? You don't regret coming?"

"It's fine. I'm extremely grateful to you."

"Don't say that. I'm not asking for gratitude."

"I don't know where else I would have gone," I said. "It was very good of you."

"It's lovely to have you. It gets very quiet here." She stretched and gave a small yawn. "It was so sudden, it must have been such a shock."

I looked through the glass doors at the gulls. They circled above where I knew the water lay, their beaks open, the cries audible.

I picked up my tea and sipped; it was still very hot.

"The money," I said. "I've given you a month's rent, in cash."

"I do trust you."

"Of course."

"So," she asked, "was it a shock?"

I tapped my fingers on the glass, then cleared my throat. "You'll let me know if you need any more money," I said.

"Andrew. It may be how you cope with it, but I'm not about to pretend nothing's happened."

The light outside was bright, clear; I leaned my forehead on the glass, concentrated on the gulls' flight, noting the pattern of their circling, the way one would suddenly plunge down to the surface of the river, then equally quickly rejoin the others.

Neither of us spoke for a while, then she finished her tea. "I'm knackered."

"Sorry," I said. "I shouldn't have come down. You probably like to be quiet when you get home."

"It's not that. It was a busy night. The ward was full." She yawned again. "I'll see you later."

"Yes," I said. "Have a good sleep."

"I'll try. I've got a couple of days to get back to normal, then I'm on day shifts." She went to leave the room, and stopped. "I meant to ask, how are the tanks?"

"Fine."

"They've settled in?"

"As far as they can settle anywhere."

"You think they'll be happy here? They like our privet?"

I smiled. "I think so."

"Good." She nodded. "I'll see you later."

I watched her walk out of the kitchen and into the hall, then she went up the stairs, leaving me alone.

The girls would be waking up now, getting ready.

What was I doing here?

My room was silent. I sat on the chair, my hands in my lap, and looked at the small bed, the row of tanks. I turned my hands over and examined the back of them. I pinched the skin and then let it fall back, observing how it took longer now to return to normal. My shorts had ridden up and my legs looked thin, thinner even than usual. I do eat, or I try at least, though I have always had problems putting on and retaining weight. It's just my inherited metabolism. That's all.

The red numbers on the bedside clock said 7:34. The two girls would be awake and downstairs, and I wondered who would get their breakfast for them.

Rachel would be up too, having had a shower and pulled on her uniform, then combed her hair back off her face before fastening it and applying her make-up. I wondered if she had slept: perhaps she'd slept all night, a sleep as deep as death, overcome with relief at having me out of the house.

I glanced back down at my hands; they felt strange to me, heavy, the fingers long and awkward, and I was aware of them touching each other, getting in the way.

To distract myself, I considered unpacking: I had nothing else to do till two o'clock. Perhaps being at work would be better than this; I had these last weeks of term on leave – compassionate, they termed it – then there would be the whole summer holidays ahead of me, but instead of any sense of elation at the free time, there was this new feeling of space and loss.

The sun was catching the vertical blinds and I stood and pulled on the plastic chain to slide them along to the side. Outside, I could see the small back garden and common land; beyond that the wide, brown channel of the river, the tide high and the sun on the water.

I opened the window to let the fresh air in and then turned to the metal shelves. The mantid was on the moist earth floor of her tank, in her new skin, which was harder now and darker. From a small box on the nearby trolley, I took out two crickets, placed them in the tank and watched.

There was an initial rotation of the head, then she was still. Alert. One of the crickets crossed her visual field. The ommatidia turned on and off and the flickering triggered a reaction. One second I could see the cricket, then there was movement and it had gone, the actual strike too fast for my vastly inferior eyesight to register.

I closed the lid and went to the window where I watched the brown water flow by, the tide forcing it from the sea, back along the length of the river.

Rachel

When the girls left, it felt as though the slam of the door reverberated right through the house, and deep into my head. Most of the red tulip petals had fallen on to the floor and I picked them up, then carried the vase through to the kitchen. I poured the stinking green water into the sink and tipped the flowers into the bin. My head hurt, as though a metal brace was tight around my forehead.

There were still the last small fragments of china on the kitchen floor, and splashes of tea. I finished clearing up, and put the dirty towel and cloth into the washing machine. The medicine box was open on the side and I found the box of tablets, popped two of them into my palm and swallowed them with a glass of water.

I stood at the sink, my head aching, and my stomach feeling empty and nauseous. My hands smelled of bleach from the cloth, sharp and high, and I washed them, using plenty of soap. I pulled my dressing gown tight round me and retied the cord, then walked to the window.

The sun was just reaching the back wall and the top

branches of the apple tree. I thought of Grace, by the door, as she left, thought of how she must have come into my bedroom to bring me my morning drink. I had to push her out of my mind. I went through to the hall and started up the stairs.

I closed the bathroom door and turned to the mirror, tried to see myself as he would when I returned to the bedroom. I ran a fingertip along the deep lines either side of my mouth. The roots of my hair were really starting to show, and I could see them against the red-brown. One stray hair sprang up from the others, short and coarse. I pulled it out and examined the definite line between the grey and red, the pointed end uncut: another hair growing through grey.

I reached for the tweezers to pluck an eyebrow hair, but they weren't on the shelf or in the basket. Grace must have taken them; she took everything else. As I rummaged for them, I caught sight of the skin on my neck which was starting to loosen. It was clearly visible when I tipped my head at a certain angle, which I did a couple of times. I stretched my face back, smoothing out the bags under my eyes, making myself look like my idea of myself, so that the two images, interior and exterior, matched.

Behind me, in the mirror, I saw the door open, and I saw him. The dark ink of his tattoos. My stomach contracted. My hands shook and I thought I could smell the bleach on them.

'You hiding from me?'

I shook my head. 'Of course not.' My voice caught and I coughed to clear my throat.

He came closer and I looked at his bare feet. Black hairs on his toes and one bruised toenail. 'Nice house,' he said.

He walked to the window, lifted the thin curtain, stood. His torso was bare, just one of my towels wrapped round his waist. His arms and back were muscular; the black ink of one tattoo spread down his arm towards his elbow. On the other arm, the black letters of his name. The towel was pulled taut over his buttocks.

He turned to look at me and my eyes fell to avoid his, fell to the front of the towel. Then further to the floor.

'Where're the kids?'

'Gone to school.'

There was a long silence. Too long. I tightened the belt of my dressing gown. Picked off a tiny bit of fluff, rolled it between my fingertips.

'What are we gonna do now?' he asked.

'Did you want a coffee?'

He smiled. 'That'd be a start.'

He sat while I boiled the kettle and got the mugs ready. As I moved, I saw him in the edge of my vision, sitting there, still in the towel.

He said nothing, but I knew he was watching me, could sense it. I placed his coffee on the table.

'So,' he said. 'How old are they?'

'The kids?'

'The kids, yeh.'

I leaned back against the worksurface, my coffee in my hands. 'Tilly's six. Grace is fifteen.'

He nodded. 'Big gap.'

'I didn't plan it.'

He stood up, looking for something. I passed him the sugar and a spoon.

'Thanks.' He put in sugar and stirred. 'So,' he said again.

I waited. I heard a passing car, a bird outside the open back door.

'Last night you said some things.'

I shook my head and held my hand up. 'Don't. I drank too much.'

'It's okay.'

'It's not,' I said. 'It's really not.'

He shrugged and we stood there, him looking out of the window at the garden. Me trying not to look at him, but at the floor, then the wall behind him.

Eventually he looked at me. 'You didn't say anything bad. It was just about him leaving.'

I nodded.

'But you didn't say when he left.'

I shrugged. 'Recently.'

'Days? Weeks? Months?'

'Weeks. He came and got his stuff yesterday. He's renting a room from a friend of mine.'

He drank his coffee and I tried not to think of anything, just to keep my mind clear, focus on the time and how I only had an hour until I should be at work. 'I'm going to be late,' I said.

'Do you have to go?'

I nodded, then in a second something opened up and I saw myself as I'd imagined in the bathroom: from his point of view; my lined, tired face and greying hair.

'Why?'

I stared at him. 'Why what?'

He smiled. 'Were you listening?'

I shook my head. 'I don't think so.'

'What were you thinking about?'

'Nothing,' I said.

'Really? It didn't look like it. Were you thinking of last night?'

I felt the heat crawl up my neck, knew I'd started to blush. I tried to laugh but an awkward cry came out.

'No,' I said. 'I wasn't.'

'You're hopeless at hiding things.' He smiled. 'I asked you if you had to go to work.'

'Of course I do. It's my job.'

'What if you were too ill to go?'

'But I'm not.'

'They'd manage for a day without you. If you were run over, what would they do?'

I looked at the garden where the sun had reached the grass. 'I have to go,' I said.

He stepped towards me.

I went to move, to set my mug down, but he rested his hands on my shoulders and pulled me to him.

He took the mug from me and put it down, then tucked my hair behind my ears, cupped my chin and lifted my face so I met his eyes. I felt a movement in my belly, and shoved him away.

'What is it?' he said.

I shook my head. 'Too much wine.'

'What is it?' he asked again.

'Nothing. It's just I got so drunk,' I said.

'I know.'

'I shouldn't have done that.'

'Done what? What we did?'

I nodded, and he lifted my head again and kissed me, gently, pressing himself against me. I felt the movement in my belly again, a shifting, as though something was starting a new life inside me.

'Do you want me to go?' he asked.

I hesitated, then shook my head. 'No.'

'Good.'

The new life in my belly uncurled. I looked away. He reached out and turned my face to look at his. 'Why are you being like this?'

I shook my head. 'I'm not being anything.'

'You are.' I still felt the urge to pull back but he kept hold of me. 'Look at me. That's better.'

'I don't feel well,' I said.

He laughed and let go of me. 'Then you can't go to work.'

'I have to.'

He kissed me again. Longer, harder. 'Call them. Tell them you're ill.'

I shook my head.

'When you're on your deathbed, will you remember this moment, and wish you'd gone to work?'

I laughed. 'No.'

'Of course you won't. So you'll ring and tell them, won't you? Come here. There. That's it.'

The covers had slipped to the floor and I lay there, my skin cooling in the daytime air. The windows open, the sound of the traffic in the room.

I glanced over at my white uniform on its hanger, on the front of the wardrobe. My name badge and silver watch, pinned to the lapel. I looked back at his still body. His eyes were closed and there were beads of sweat on his forehead. The sight of him in there, in my bed, was like a physical shock; I'd had sixteen years of seeing the same body – such a different body – next to me.

I touched his shoulder, traced the pattern of the tattoo with my finger. Ran it up and down each of the letters. His name. D–A–V–E. And the Latin inscription: *Carpe Diem*. The room smelled of the fresh summer air, but also of us.

The phone rang and I went to get out of bed to answer it. 'Don't,' he said. 'It could be your work.'

I waited, and the ringing went on and on, then finally stopped.

He turned towards me. 'Did you ever imagine this?'

'What?' I asked.

'Don't play games. Did you?'

'I'm not telling you,' I said.

'I did,' he said. 'I used to watch you with the other patients and I'd be waiting for you to come to me.'

'Stop it,' I said.

'Don't you believe it?'

'No,' I said. 'Of course not.'

'Why?'

'Why would you want to look at me?'

'Don't say that. Why d'you think so little of yourself?'

'I don't know.' A dog barked outside, and a bird flew past the window.

'Come on. Tell me.'

'I feel bad,' I said.

'Why?'

'You know why.'

'Because of him only leaving recently?'

'Partly.'

'What else? Drinking too much? Doing what we did?'

I said nothing.

'Or was it your daughter coming in and seeing me?'

'Maybe,' I said.

'Oh, come on. It's natural, there's nothing wrong with it. Anyway, you need a life.'

'Maybe,' I said. I turned away from him and saw the time. The girls would be at school now. Grace in her classroom, the anger still hot inside her. At least she was going to Andrew's today, not coming back here, not forcing me to face her.

Andrew would be there, in the house by the river. And here I was, here in the warm room, with this man.

'Rachel.'

'What?'

'You talked a lot last night.'

'Did I?'

'Yeh. You said a lot of things.'

He touched my shoulder, pulled me round to face him.

'Don't start that again,' he said. 'Not looking at me, going silent on me.'

'I don't remember what I said.'

'On the way home, by the river.'

As he said the words an image came to me, of the two of us, arm in arm, walking by the water. None of what we said stayed with me, just the pressure of his arm round my shoulder and the way his hip had moved against mine, and then him pushing me up against the fence and kissing me, touching me. As I recalled it, the feeling from earlier, of some new growth inside me, returned.

'I asked you if you were happy,' he reminded me.

'What did I say?'

'You said no. You said you hadn't been happy for a long time.'

'I don't remember that.'

'Are you happy now?'

'Now?'

'Here and now, yes.'

'I don't know,' I said. 'I feel bad, about Grace. And about him. Andrew.'

'But what about me?' he said. 'Do you wish I'd just gone this morning?'

'No.'

'Well, that's something.'

'I'm glad you're here,' I said. 'Of course I am, but I don't know why you'd want to be.'

He sat up and took my hand in his. 'You have to stop this. You need more confidence. I'm here because I wanted to do this from when I first met you, and I think you're beautiful.'

'No,' I said. 'I know I'm not.'

'Why are you like this?' he asked. 'You have to stop it.' His voice was firm, emphatic. 'I don't want to hear it. I know it's not ideal, they shouldn't have found us, but we're human beings, that's all, and we both needed this. Are you listening?'

'Yes,' I said.

'I don't believe you.'

I looked him straight in the eye.

'That's better. No more of that rubbish. You agree?'

'I'll try,' I said.

'I think you're beautiful. You can look away all you like but I won't stop telling you.' He ran his finger along my profile, down my nose, round my chin. 'You believe me?'

I nodded. 'If I have to.'

'You do.' He lay back against his pillows and smiled.

'When you nursed me, I bet you came home and thought about me. Bet you'd be here next to him, comparing us.'

I slapped him lightly. 'Stop it.'

'You did, didn't you? I know you did.'

'Stop it.'

'Not till you admit it.'

'What should I admit?'

'That you thought of me like that.'

'I think of everyone I look after.'

He rolled me over on to my back, straddled me, pinned my arms by my sides. 'You did, didn't you?'

I laughed. 'All right. I did.'

He let go. 'That's better.'

We lay, me in his arms, and listened to the birds outside, the cars, voices in the street.

'When do the kids get back?' he asked.

'He's collecting them.'

'Is he bringing them here?'

'No. They're going to his house.'

'That's okay then. You get an evening off, and it's not like he's on his own.'

'No. True.'

'Did he want to leave you?' he asked.

'No. I asked him to. To try and move on.'

'I see.'

'Have you ever been married?' I asked.

He laughed. 'No. Not even come close.'

'Why not?'

'Could never find the right person, I suppose.'

There was a long pause, then I spoke. 'Don't you have to go to work?'

He shook his head. 'They'll manage.' He ran a finger along my collarbone. 'And don't start that again, that you have to. If you try and leave I'll lock you in. I'm planning to be here all day with you.'

I opened my mouth to ask why, then stopped myself. Because he wanted to, because he found me beautiful. That was what he had said.

'We'll always remember this. The two of us in your bed with the sun and the open window.'

I nodded.

'We're very lucky.'

'Yes,' I said, 'we are.' And I thought yes, I am lucky, to feel this at my age, when I thought it had all gone.

'Rachel, do you want some coffee?'

I moved as if to get up.

'No. I'll do it.'

'You don't know where anything is.'

'I'm sure I can find it.' He grinned. 'I've made coffee before.' He left the room, closing the door behind him.

I lifted my arm and smelled my skin, then bent over and smelled the pillow next to me. The smell of him. I thought of what he had said, that we would always remember this day.

The touch of him on my body, the feel of his skin on mine.

For sixteen years it had been the same body next to me in the bed. The same pale skin and thin hair. Tentative hands reaching out. The featherlightness of his fingertips.

And this man, so different. The man who, yes, I *had* thought about when I looked after him, when I changed him and dressed his wounds, washed dried blood from his scar. Who I hadn't seen again until last night, when he had walked into the pub and seen me across the crowds.

But this morning and Grace coming into the room and seeing him. My stomach contracted.

I got out of the bed and took my dressing gown off the door, covered myself up. I sat back on the bed and waited for him to come back.

Tilly

I like looking out of the window. The clouds chase each other. Clouds are full of water and they are born in the rivers.

When the teacher wants us to be quiet she rings a bell. And when we have to go and eat she rings a bell. If she doesn't ring the bell we can't do it.

My bag hangs on a hook at school. My name is on a piece of card under the hook so I know it's mine. My book was in my bag and I couldn't really see it, but if I closed my eyes I could. I had pictures of it inside my head. Pictures of the pictures. And pictures of the words. I can read it but I like it best when Grace reads it to me and then I can listen.

There is one picture I love. The box is being opened and I can see Manty's face looking out at her new home. Her head is a triangle, only it is upside down.

I can hang upside down from the swing in the garden. The blood sinks to my head and I go pink in the face. It is the blood which makes me pink. My head gets full of it.

I wonder if praying mantises are full of blood. Or water. Or sticky juice. My dad would know. He would tell me the answer then check in one of his books. And he would show me the answer and I know he would be right. But his books are at my house and he isn't.

The Unhappy Insect

Manty looked around her new tank. There was no lovely soft earth. No lovely green leaves.

The floor of the tank was covered in dead leaves. There was one stick, but it was old and dry. And instead of a nice clean water bowl there was the lid of a jam jar.

The glass of the tank was streaked and dirty.

Manty wanted to curl up and die.

All she could think of was her old tank, and her old life.

She took a sip from the stale water and waited.

When the lid of the tank opened, a large hairy hand appeared. Manty buried herself in the dead leaves and hid.

Grace

I left him there on the ground under the tree, in the dead leaves, and ran out into the sun, crossed the field to the road.

I followed the dog, both of us running, and saw an isolated red-brick farmhouse on the high ground of the river bank. The dog ran straight through the yard to the back door.

I knocked and shouted but no one answered. I tried the handle but the door was locked. I ran round to the front door and again knocked and shouted. Still no one. There was a glass panel and I could see the key in the lock. I looked for something heavy. Picked up a brick from the front garden and tapped it against the glass. It didn't break at first so I hit harder until it broke. I made a hole big enough to put my arm through without cutting myself, then reached in and grasped the key, turned it. I put my shoulder against the door to open it, but it wouldn't give. I stepped back and kicked and it flew open, banging back against the wall.

I stood in the hall, the stairs to my left. I looked around

for the phone, taking in the dark brown woodwork, the worn floorboards. And the walls. Bare plaster, covered in writing. I didn't stop to look at what the words said, but ran from the hall into the kitchen, saw that beyond lay the scullery and back door. I retraced my steps back to the hall and went through the other door, into the living room. No phone. I went out into the hallway, again seeing the writing on the walls, the bare plaster. Then I saw it, on the bookcase at the bottom of the stairs. I picked up the receiver and sat down on the bottom step to try to catch my breath.

They answered quickly and I asked for an ambulance. Told them what I had seen, where I was, who I was. I asked if I should go back to the man under the tree, but they said to wait for them to show them where he lay.

I put the receiver down, letting it rest in its heavy, old-fashioned cradle. The muscles in my legs were stinging from running, and the very bottom of my lungs ached. I sat there a while, my head resting on my legs, recovering.

After a while I lifted my head and looked about me. The dark woodwork, bare floorboards, old round light switches, a circular mirror on the wall which distorted what it reflected.

And on each wall, there were the words I had seen.

They ran along the top of the skirting, around the door frames, and above the picture rail, the free and elegant letters nearly touching the ceiling. The ink was jet black, except for the initial letters, which were larger than the others and filled in with silver, gold, red, blue.

I read the words by the skirting board. *The earth is the*

Lord's. And then around the door frame: *He causeth the grass to grow for the cattle, and herb for the service of man.*

I heard the back door open and stood up, walked towards the kitchen. A woman emerged from the scullery. She wore a woollen hat pulled tightly over her grey hair, a bunch of leaves in her hand.

I pointed to the hallway. —I had to call an ambulance, I said. —It was an emergency.

She moved towards me. —Get out, she said. —Get out.

I shook my head. —No. I have to wait for the ambulance.

—What ambulance? she asked. Then she looked down at the dog, back up at me. Looked at me differently, her voice lower, quieter. —What's happened?

—I found someone hurt. A man. He sent me here to get help.

—What man? she asked.

—I don't know. I didn't know him, I said.

She took a photograph down from the wall and showed it to me. —Is this him? Is it David? My son, David?

I nodded. —Yes.

—Where is he? We have to go to him.

—I can't, I said. —They told me to wait here. I have to show them where to go.

She stared at me, then her upper body folded over suddenly, as though I had hit her. I helped her to a chair and sat her down. The dog lay under the table, by her feet.

I took a glass from the draining board and filled it with water, put it on the table in front of her.

She sat there, her eyes closed, the glass of water untouched. I read the words round the kitchen window: *Will I eat the flesh of bulls, or drink the blood of goats?*

I looked at the photograph which lay in her lap. Words ran round the outside of the frame, *Kiss the son lest he be angry.* Inside, the face of the young man, short pale hair. Blue eyes.

I heard the siren, quiet at first, then louder as it neared us. I ran out of the front door and stood in the road to flag it down. They opened the door for me to get in, and helped the woman through the back door, then we drove off quickly. I directed them to where I had emerged from the woods, and we parked. They unloaded a stretcher and bag and I led them across the field and through the trees to the clearing.

I stood back as they ran forward to examine him. The woman caught up with them and fell to her knees next to her son. They strapped him on to the stretcher. I looked up through branches and leaves, at the pieces of sky. The end of the rope.

—Grace, the driver said. —You have to come with us.

I followed them through the trees, out to the field. A police car was parked next to the ambulance, and a WPC walked towards us. The driver spoke to her quickly, and she led me to her car. The stretcher was loaded into the back of the ambulance and they closed the doors and drove off, the siren sounding in the hot air.

—Are you all right? the woman asked.

I nodded. —I think so.

—It must have been a shock.

I nodded again.

—Your father's on his way. We called your mother's work, but she's off ill.

—She's not ill, I said.

—Well, I tried your home number, but there was no answer.

She opened the car door and I got in, rested my head back. I tucked my hands between my knees to stop them shaking, and I waited for Dad.

We drove towards the town, along the path of the river. I put my window down and stared out at the willows along the river bank. Neither of us spoke for a while.

Eventually, he broke the silence. —Why weren't you at school?

I watched a house flash by, then a field full of yellow dandelions.

—Grace? Are you going to answer?

I said nothing and we passed another house, went over the bridge.

—Grace, he said again, —I asked you a question.

I turned my head slightly towards him and examined his profile. His thinning blond hair falling on to his face, his large nostrils, the nose hairs poking out.

He glanced at me and I quickly looked away.

—I think I know him, he said, —I think I used to teach him. Did they tell you his surname?

—No.

—I taught a David who lived in one of these houses by the river. He was lucky you found him.

—It was the dog who did it, I said. —It wasn't me.

—Lucky that the dog found you then. But I still want to know what you were doing there. Why you weren't at school. Grace? There must be a reason.

I shifted towards the door and rested my weight on it. The lock was down, but I tried to imagine what might happen if it wasn't. If the door hadn't quite closed and my weight forced it to swing open. Which part of me would hit the road first? My head? My upper body, scraping on the tarmac? I closed my eyes but the image was replaced by David's face in the dead leaves. The dirt on his pale skin. The oddly sized pupils as he looked at me.

Dad cleared his throat. —Your mother isn't at home or work.

—I know, I said.

—They said she'd called in sick. Did she seem ill to you?

—No.

—Strange. I don't understand.

—We're not going to the house now, are we? I asked.

—No. Why?

—I don't want to.

—What is it? he asked. —What's going on?

—Nothing, I said. —Absolutely nothing.

But all I could think of was her and that man in the house, and us going there and Dad finding them together.

We went over the next bridge and I looked at the river beneath us. The water was thick, brown.

Dad parked in the town centre and turned the engine off. A woman was struggling to fold up her double buggy to get it into her car.

—It must've been a terrible shock, he said, —finding him like that.

I said nothing.

—A terrible shock. If he is the boy I remember, he was always very quiet, came from an odd family. He tapped the clock on the dashboard. —Look at the time. Have you eaten?

—No.

—You must be hungry. I'll go and get some food, and by the time we've eaten it, Tilly'll be due out. Then we'll go back to Barbara's.

I watched him walk across the car park towards the shops. His thin legs in his shorts. His hair that flopped up and down as he walked.

I leaned back and closed my eyes. Images from the morning came to me: one man's skin and his tattoos, the dark ink letters on the white; the younger man's face, his legs in the dead leaves. The rope hanging from the tree. And the words threading their way round the window of the kitchen in the farmhouse. *Will I eat the flesh of bulls, or drink the blood of goats?*

I opened my eyes. Noticed the windscreen was covered in flat insect bodies, tiny smears of red and green.

—Grace.

I turned. Dad's face at the car window.

—Come on, he said. —We'll go and sit by the river.

I got out and followed him back along the road, over the bridge and on to the footpath.

The tide was beginning to recede and the water was moving towards the sea. We sat on a bench and Dad spread the food out between us and gave me a drink.

We sat there silently and I watched the water. Dad opened a sandwich and took just one bite, then put it back.

—I thought, he said, —you were staying over. You don't have your stuff.

—No, I said.

—I don't understand. She said she'd give it to you to take to school. We'll have to go to the house to get it.

I looked at the sandwiches and then at the water.

—I'm not going there.

He turned towards me. —Why?

I stood and walked towards the river, picked up a small stone and threw it in.

—Why? What is it?

I threw another stone.

—What the hell is going on? Grace?

I shrugged and bent down for another stone.

—It's nothing, I said, but I could tell he didn't believe me. We stayed there a while, then he put his sandwich in the bin.

—Come on, let's go and get Tilly.

What is man, that thou art mindful of him? and the son of man,
that thou visitest him?

For thou hast made him a little lower than the angels,
and hast crowned him with glory and honour.

Thou madest him to have dominion over the works of thy hands;
thou has put all things under his feet:

All sheep and oxen, yea, and the beasts of the field;

The fowl of the air, and the fish of the sea, and whatsoever
passeth through the paths of the seas.

Grace

The sun was bright and I watched Tilly walk towards the car, her book bag and lunch box in her hands. She went to the back door and opened it, got in.

Dad started the engine.

—Where are we going? Tilly asked.

Dad sighed. —I've told you over and over. You know where we're going.

He drove over the bridge and out of the town, towards Barbara's.

—Why have we got to go to her house? Tilly asked.

Dad lifted his hand and slammed it down on the steering wheel impatiently. —Tilly, how many times have I told you? You know why.

—But why've you got a new house?

—That's enough, Dad said.

Tilly sat in silence for a while, then started again. —Where's Mum?

I stared straight ahead. Dad said nothing.

—Where's Mum?

I turned round and saw that Tilly lay on the back seat, her shoes off, her bare feet resting against the window. She glanced at me and flicked her eyes away quickly.

—Where're your socks? I asked.

She stared at me, then moved her feet, leaving imprints of them on the glass. She spoke, each word clear and firm.

—Mum has a man in the house, she said.

Silence in the car.

Dad reached down and took a cloth and wiped the windscreen even though it wasn't steamed up or anything.

Tilly's voice again. Each word as clear as before.

—She has a man in the house and he sleeps in your bed.

I opened the car door and Tilly climbed over on to my seat to get out. We followed Dad into the house.

Barbara was in the kitchen. She smiled as we walked in.
—Hi, Grace. Hi, Tilly.

I smiled and said hello. Tilly just stared at her and Barbara smiled again, less confidently this time.

—Are you all right, Tilly? she asked.

—No, Tilly said. —Why've I got to come here?

Barbara looked at Dad, but he walked off.

—Why've I got to come here? Tilly asked again.

—Because your dad's come to live here, Barbara said.
—He's sharing this house.

Tilly glared at her, then ran past me through the doors into the garden.

—You okay, Grace? Barbara asked.

—Yeh, I said. —I'm all right.

I looked out, watched Tilly in the garden. Her skirt blew against her legs, and leaves flew through the air.

—I've got some stuff to eat, Barbara said. —Your dad gave me a list of what you both like.

—Right, I said.

—So. Your dad told me what happened, you finding that man. Is he all right, do you know?

I shrugged. —They took him off this morning in the ambulance.

—Do you know anything about him?

—He's called David. Dad thinks he taught him.

She nodded. —He was so lucky you were there.

—I know.

—What were you doing there, Grace? You should have been at school.

—I know, I said. —But I wasn't. Okay?

She said my name again, her voice calm and trying to be kind. I ignored her and followed Tilly into the garden. I could see the river. It was so wide here, a sheet of brown water at high tide, and a sheet of silt at low tide, with a thin ribbon of water in the centre.

Tilly was sitting on the river bank. I sat by her and she rested her head against me. A woman walked by, three dogs at her feet.

—I want to go home, Tilly said.

I put my arm round her. —I know.

—Don't like it here. It's too wet.

—The house isn't wet, I said.

—It feels it.

I heard Dad calling us, but I didn't move. Tilly jumped up and ran off.

I watched the seagulls for a while, circling above the water. Then I went back inside. Taking an apple from the table, I walked into the hall and climbed the stairs, follow- ing the sound of Tilly's voice. Dad's room was at the rear of the house, and painted green and white. He'd put the shelves along one wall and there were leads and plugs and sockets everywhere. Tilly stood on a chair, peering into one of the tanks.

—Here, Dad said. —Now stand nice and quietly and you can watch her eat it.

I looked round the room. He'd unpacked some of the books on to the shelves, but there was still a pile of boxes.

—How long are you staying here? I asked.

—Not sure. He grabbed Tilly's hand. —Don't tap the tank.

—Are you staying long?

He shrugged. —It depends. I don't really know. Barbara says I can stay as long as I need.

—I'm sure she does, I said.

He stared at me. —What's that mean?

Tilly jumped up and down with excitement. —He's eaten it.

—*She*, Tilly, Dad said. —It's a female. He turned back to me. —What do you mean, Grace?

—Nothing, I said.

—Does she swallow all of it? Tilly asked. —Even the eyes?

—If it's a small insect, yes.

Tilly smiled at me. —She ate it, Grace.

—I know, I said.

—Look, Dad said to me. —I know it's not ideal. None of this is ideal.

—What's she doing now? Tilly asked.

—I don't know. I could heard his voice getting tight and angry.

I kicked at one of the boxes. —I hate this house.

—That's not what you said when you came before.

—That was different. I picked up the book by the bed and flicked through the pages. There was a photograph of a large adult mantid on a twig, its eyes bulging. —They're disgusting creatures, I said. —I don't know why you keep them.

—Don't say that, Tilly said. —You'll upset Dad. She rubbed Dad's arm. —I like them.

—I know, he said.

I closed the book and placed it down.

—Where's my room? Tilly asked.

—I'll show you, Dad said.

Our room was up a small wooden staircase, like a ladder, at the very top of the house. The ceiling sloped and there were two skylights. Two single beds.

—You expect me to share with Tilly? I asked.

—It's just for now. Just until I can sort something out.

He touched the duvet cover. —Look, Barbara's got you all new bedding organized.

Tilly climbed on to one of the beds and began to bounce on it. —I want this one.

Dad grabbed her arm. —Don't do that.

—I'm not sharing a room with her, I said.

—Why not? he asked.

—Because I'm not, I said. —I don't know why I've got to stay here anyway.

—Because that was what was agreed.

—Who by? I asked. —Who agreed it? I didn't.

Tilly was still bouncing on the bed. Dad grabbed her arm again. —Look, Grace, he said, —if you don't stay here I won't see you.

—I'm not something to be moved from house to house, I said.

—That's not what we're doing. He turned to Tilly. — Please will you stop that.

—This is all just so stupid, I said.

—Do you think I don't know that? he shouted.

I said nothing, just stared at him.

—I'm sorry, he said. —I didn't mean to shout.

—Then don't, I said, and I walked out. I heard him call my name, but took no notice, went down the stairs.

Barbara called out from the kitchen. —That you, Andy?

I stood in the kitchen doorway. —No, I said. —It's me.

—Oh, she said. —Hi, Grace. Did he show you the room? It's not perfect, but it's something.

I nodded. —Thanks.

—I know it's all difficult for you, she said. —And I'm really sorry.

I shrugged.

—I hope you know you can talk to me. Whenever you want.

—I've got nothing to say.

—Not now, but you may do one day. How is she?

—Who?

—You know who I mean. Your mum.

I shrugged. —I don't know.

—Grace, she said. —Sit down. I'll make some tea and we can have a chat.

I shook my head. —No. I'm gonna go out for a bit.

—Where?

—I just need to get some air.

I walked to the end of the road, to the old boatyard. A few small boats were up on the silt, their bottoms stained brown. Another, larger boat lay on its side.

I continued till I reached the fields and could no longer see any houses, then sat down by the bank. The grass was dry and smelled of summer. Cows in the next field watched me over the hedge.

I lay back and closed my eyes, felt the light of the sun through the thin skin of my eyelids.

I thought of the house where David lived, with its red-brick walls and slate roof. The garden stretching right to the river. I imagined slipping into the muddy water here at the river's mouth, and swimming upriver, away from the sea, until I reached the end of his garden. I imagined climbing out, my body wet and tired, and walking along the path to the back of the house. I would wipe the dust on the window and look in and see the table and chairs, dirty plates on the table, a loaf of white bread on the board. And I would see the walls. *Deliver my soul from the sword; my darling from the power of the dog.* And the photograph of him, his pale skin and the frame. *Kiss the son lest he be angry.*

I sat up and opened my eyes. The light had blurred my vision. I waited until it cleared before taking my sandals off and creeping closer to the water. I lay down and reached a toe down, feeling the cold of it.

The sky was so blue, the sun hot. I thought of the room with its sloping ceiling and attic windows. The two thin mattresses.

I thought of Mum's room, at the top of the house, the light staining the room pink through the red curtains.

I didn't want another house, another room. Didn't want any of this.

I closed my eyes again and thought of when I had known which bed I was in, and knew who was in the other beds. When Tilly would come to me in the morning, climb in beside me, smelling of her own room and of the night. And Dad would bring us tea and then make breakfast before walking us to school. And on Sunday evenings we would wash our hair and dry it downstairs, me combing Tilly's hair, her hot body leaning into mine, her breathing heavy.

On the way back to the house, I saw something move at the side of the road, in the long grass. I bent down and looked more closely. It was grey, formless, and it took a moment to realize it was a small bird. I picked it up and held it carefully. It was still warm and I looked up into the tree for a nest, but could see nothing.

I cupped it in my hands and started walking quickly towards the house. Dad was outside.

—Where've you been? he asked.

—For a walk, I said.

He nodded and smiled. —I've got some good news. The police just called. They said David is going to be fine.

I nodded. —Good.

—And he is the boy I taught.

—You've taught everyone, I said.

He smiled again. —It must seem like it. Anyway, they told me where he is if you'd like to visit him. Do you want to?

I nodded. —I think so, yes.

—Good. I'll take you there. He saw I was holding something. —What have you got?

I opened my hands. He took it from me, turned it over, examining it.

—Be careful, I said.

—It's all right. I know what I'm doing.

He gave it back and I felt the skin on its belly, the beat of its heart.

—It's a wood pigeon, he said. —It's very young. I don't think it'll survive.

—I'm going to care for it, I said.

—Well, don't be disappointed. You mustn't be upset if it doesn't make it.

I said nothing, looked down at it in my hands, its huge beak and tiny, featherless head.

—You understand? he said. —It's nearly impossible to raise them from this young, and you don't know how damaged it is from falling out of the nest.

—It doesn't look damaged.

—I know, he said. —But prepare yourself. You know what you're like. You know you get so involved.

Yes, I thought, I know what I'm like. I get so involved. So involved.

I found a box and lined it with soft tissue, then put it into the airing cupboard. Dad showed me how to soak brown bread in water and feed the bird tiny pellets. I had to force its beak open and place the bread at the back of its mouth and it would swallow. That night I went to bed and tried not to think about it, but when I woke later, the moonlight shining through the skylight on to my face, I took the box from the cupboard and carried it down to the kitchen.

I was scared to look, knowing I would find its hard

body lying on one side, its eye blank. But I made myself lift the flaps and there it was, waiting for food, eyeing me beadily.

David was asleep. He was propped against the pillows and his hair was almost red next to the white cotton. His skin was a different colour now, brighter, and he wore a blue tee-shirt. His arms were slightly tanned and freckled.

By the bed there was a trolley with a half-eaten plate of food. The remains of a jacket potato, and some grated cheese. A small salad garnish, the cress scattered over the plate. The bed opposite was empty but there were flowers and a few cards on the table. In the third bed there was a middle-aged man who was reading a newspaper. He lowered it and smiled at me.

I looked away. Looked at the shape David's body made under the bedclothes. I stared at his face and wondered if he would sense me watching him and wake. If he didn't, I'd have to write a note for him. Just as I looked around to see if there was a pen, he moved. His eyes opened and he focused on me. I smiled, but he didn't respond.

—D'you know who I am? I asked.

He nodded. —In the woods.

—The police told me you were here, I said. —They said I could come and see you.

He nodded again.

—I just wanted to make sure you were okay. I brought you these.

I picked up the chocolates I'd bought on my way in and

gave them to him. I sat there for a while, not knowing what to say.

—I must have fallen asleep, he said. —Was I asleep when you came in?

—I think so.

—You should have woken me.

—I didn't like to, I said.

He stared at me. —I thought I remembered you, he said, —but I've been confused. I wasn't sure if you were real.

I smiled. —I am, I said.

He played with the frayed edge of the blanket.

—My dad drove me, I said. —He's waiting outside in the car. I just wanted to say hello.

He nodded. —I should say thank you, he said. —For finding me. But I don't know if I mean it.

I looked at the marks on his neck, dark bruises now.

—You don't have to say anything, I said. —It was the dog who fetched me anyway.

He nodded, and I stood up ready to leave.

—Grace, he said. —It is Grace?

—Yeh.

—I thought it was. Thank you for coming.

—That's okay.

I stood there for a few moments, then walked out, through the ward, back along the corridors.

The Unhappy Insect

Manty crept out from the dead leaves to see what the hairy hand had put in the tank.

She was so hungry her stomach was rumbling, but there was only one dead cricket.

Manty didn't like to eat dead crickets. She ate live ones that still hopped and chirruped.

So Manty waited. The next day the same thing happened. The lid was lifted and the hairy hand appeared. Manty hid and waited till she heard the lid go down.

Another dead cricket.

Manty was getting thin now, and very, very unhappy. She looked out of the dirty glass. The room was full of tanks on metal shelves. She looked up at the lid. Maybe she could push it off and escape.

She got on to her back legs and tried to climb the glass, but her feet just slid down hopelessly.

Manty tried one more time, but she still kept sliding down and fell and landed on the dry leaves. Poor Manty. She didn't know what to do.

Andrew

I set out very early, before the sun had entirely risen over the horizon. My bag contained a large bottle of water and a notebook and automatic pencil. I had also packed two apples and the large-scale map of the area, along with my small compass.

I walked along the course of the river, observing where it had sliced into the land, carving its route. It was low tide and the initial section was thick silt, covered in the pronged fork-like footprints of the gulls which circled overhead, cut through by a small flow of water.

The old boatyard was empty and quiet; a black dog was standing by a small boat, stranded on the estuarine mud. There was a warmth in the air, even at this early hour, and I took off my lightweight jacket. Birds circled in the air, calling out the new day, and I unthreaded their calls, identifying them. Gull, thrush, blackbird. I passed the verge where the previous week Grace had found the wood pigeon which, to my surprise, was still alive, growing and filling out. I craned my head, tried to see a nest in the branches above, but couldn't.

I climbed the gate ahead of me, into the first field outside the village. The grass was trodden flat, a path marked out by previous walkers. I stepped up on to the bank; the water was heavy with coloration from the mud. I stopped for a moment, sitting on the dry grass, watching for any visiting wildlife. It was a simple landscape, primitive even: the silt, the water, the grass and the vast blue sky, in which there was absolutely no trace of white, not even a cirrus cloud.

I lay back and tried to focus on the detail of the grasses around me, hoping to spot any new varieties, or some insects, but my mind began to drift and I couldn't stop thinking about it all, from the first two weeks in the bed and breakfast, to Barbara offering her room and my subsequent return to the house to pack up my boxes. And then the first visit from the girls. And of course, under all this, beating out an unbearable rhythm, the words Tilly had uttered in the car. "She has a man in the house and he sleeps in your bed."

My eyes were watering, the light from the new sun harsh. I shifted to the side, my cheek resting on the grass, the smell of the earth rising into my nostrils. I wiped my eyes with my bare arm.

"She has a man in the house and he sleeps in your bed."

Our bed, chosen and bought by the two of us. A large, expensive bed, with a thick mattress. An adult bed. A marriage bed. I wiped my eyes again and stood up. I felt oddly light-headed, my legs weak, as though I was about to slip and spill into the river. I turned towards the village and started walking slowly along the river bank.

The post was piled on the doormat. I placed Barbara's letters on the hall table and carried the one addressed to me up into my room. I closed the door firmly and sat on the bed before I opened it. I recognized the fine black pen and sloped letters, as well as the yellow envelopes Rachel used. I examined it carefully, first the front then the back. I actually put my finger under the partly sealed flap of the envelope, when some impulse made me stop. I looked at the envelope one more time, then placed it on the bed. I walked to the window and looked out towards the river. The gulls circled, screaming.

In the tank the mantid was rigidly still, her front legs folded and raised as though in prayer, her new skin hard now, complete. I placed one small cricket in the tank, and watched for the almost imperceptible movement of the mantid's head as her compound eye caught sight of the insect and its image was magnified and multiplied, each image from a slightly different angle. She waited, rigid, ready to strike.

Quickly, before I could think about it, I snatched up the yellow envelope and ripped it open. I pulled out a card, an image of a beach, the waves high and fierce. Inside, in Rachel's distinctive handwriting, a plea to meet to discuss the children and our arrangements in an amicable fashion. That we should remain friends for their sake.

Back in the tank the mantid remained still, but the cricket had gone.

I heard the bedroom door opposite mine open and close, followed by the sound of Barbara making her way along the landing and down the stairs. I sprayed the tanks to moisten the soil, then picked up Rachel's card and ripped it into pieces. I placed them carefully in the bin.

By the time I joined her in the kitchen, Barbara was at the table, a slice of toast in front of her. She looked up and smiled.

"Ah," I said, "you're up and about."

"You know I am," she said. "You heard me, then waited a bit before coming down."

"Did I?"

She laughed. "You know you did." She took the lid off the butter dish. "You're very easy to read."

"Am I?"

"You are, yes." She started buttering her toast. "You know something? You can be very funny."

"Can I?"

She nodded. "Maybe that was the problem. Rachel's never had a great sense of humour."

"Hasn't she?" I asked.

"Have you never noticed?"

"I'm beginning to think I haven't noticed anything."

"That would explain a lot." She laughed again.

I walked to the fridge and opened it. "I'm glad," I said, "that I am providing some kind of entertainment for you."

"Andrew. Don't be like that."

I found an open packet of bacon and a box of eggs. "Like what?" I asked.

"Like this. I'm not laughing *at* you."

"Has it occurred to you," I said, "that though you think I'm easy to read, there may be occasions when I would prefer people not to read me?"

She waited a while before saying, "Yes. But I can't pretend not to see what I see. You know what I'm like, how direct I am. Sorry."

I felt the shell of the egg in my hand and for a moment I imagined it soft and malleable, as it had been when it passed from the chicken and into the cold, hardening air. I felt its weight in my hand, then I don't know what happened. I heard a voice calling my name but it wasn't clear and I didn't know where it came from. My heart was beating impossibly fast and I found breathing difficult. Then the voice came again. I looked down: shell and yolk and albumen mixed together on the floor. I felt an arm on mine.

I turned and leaned over the sink, rested my head on my arms. I could hear loud breaths, but it took a few moments to realize they came from deep inside my own body. They slowly quietened.

"Andrew?"

I took the kitchen roll and bent down to clear up the egg.

"Let me," Barbara said.

"No."

The word, spoken too loud, too forcefully, ricocheted, then settled into a long silence in the room.

Eventually she asked if I was okay.

"I'm fine," I said. "I dropped an egg, that's all."

She watched as I picked up the shell and mopped up the rest. I put the kitchen towel into the bin and opened the fridge again, to take out a second egg.

"Shall I cook for you?"

"No," I said. "I am able to cook for myself."

There was another silence. I took out a pan and placed it on the hob. The heat spread through the oil and the bacon lost its translucency and became a deep pink. I added a drop more oil and cracked the egg on the side. My hands shook slightly and a tiny fragment of shell fell into the pan. I went to fish it out, not thinking about the heat. It took a while to register the pain, and by the time I examined the end of my finger, the skin was red and smooth.

I slipped the bacon and egg on to the plate, and grabbed a knife and fork, took them to the table. I seasoned the egg with freshly ground black pepper and cut the bacon. Barbara stood up, got some bread and dropped it into the toaster. I placed the first forkful in my mouth; the bacon tasted salty, and the white of the egg was not quite cooked and its gelatinous texture nearly made me retch. I forced myself to chew then swallow. The food felt odd in my mouth: a foreign object.

The last click of the toaster sounded and Barbara put one slice in front of me, the other on her plate.

"Are you all right now?" she asked as she sat down.

I nodded and swallowed the small fragment of bacon which I'd been pushing around my mouth with the end of my tongue. "Fine."

"What was it? Was it what I said?"

"I don't want to discuss it," I said.

"Okay."

I cleaned my knife on the toast before I buttered it, careful to spread right up to the crusts. I took one bite.

"Andrew," Barbara said. She waited until I looked at her, then she continued. "I'm sorry. I made fun of you and I shouldn't have. I was insensitive and it's too early." She put her hand out towards mine, which rested on the table. "Can we start again?"

"What would we start again?"

"You know what."

"If it makes you feel better," I said.

"Good. So. How's the toast?"

"Like toast."

She smiled and stood up to put the kettle on. I set down my knife and pushed my plate away, the remains of the breakfast making me feel sick.

Barbara turned. "What are you going to do today? You are getting them from school?"

"Yes."

"And dropping them off?"

I nodded. "I am, yes."

"And how's Grace?"

I heard myself sigh. "She missed school again. I've asked them to call me any time she doesn't turn up."

"Do you know where she's going?"

"No."

"Have you tried talking to her?"

"No."

"Andy. You have to talk to her."

"I don't know what to say."

"Is she talking to her mother?"

"I don't know," I said.

Barbara poured the water into the teapot, then brought it to the table.

"Grace barely speaks to me," I said.

"It's a difficult time for her."

We sat there while Barbara poured the tea. She sat back in her chair and regarded me keenly, then, "We never understood her choosing you. No one did."

She pushed my mug towards me.

"I don't mean that there was anything wrong with you. It was just you didn't seem like the man she would choose to live with. You're just such different people."

"Lots of people are," I said.

"I know, but they don't live together."

"No."

"Andrew," she said. "What are you going to do now?"

I shook my head. "I don't know."

"You need something."

"I have the children."

"But they're at school most days, and you don't have them all the time." She waited, but I didn't respond. "Look," she said, "you can stay here as long as you want. It's not that.

It's just that I don't know what'll happen to you if you sit around here all day, waiting for them to finish school, dwelling on everything."

I still didn't respond.

She pointed at my breakfast plate. "You have to eat. You're losing weight."

"Am I?"

"You know you are. You need food."

"I know what I need," I said, the words louder and sharper than I had intended.

She frowned. "You're not waiting for her to change her mind, are you? Are you?"

I picked up my plate and mug and walked to the sink.

"Andrew?"

I turned around. "When did you last see her?" I asked.

She looked away. "Yesterday."

"Did she ask how I was?" I noticed Barbara purse her lips a fraction. "Well? Did she?"

"I wasn't there long. I just called in for five minutes."

"I see."

"Andrew."

I concentrated on scraping the uneaten food from my plate into the bin. Streaks of egg yolk ran down the white china.

"I talked to her about Grace," Barbara said. "I said she was clearly unhappy. She changed the subject and talked about . . ."

"What?" I asked. "What did she talk about?"

"She talked about work."

I stared at her. "I think you were about to say something else."

She shook her head. "Do you think I shouldn't see her?"

I shrugged. "I don't know. You're her friend." I waited a bit, then asked, "Has she said why?"

It was a while before she said anything and I could sense her forming responses and rejecting them. Eventually she spoke: "I think she wanted the marriage to end."

"Yes," I said. "I'm not sure how helpful it is to state the obvious."

"No."

"You know, Barbara," I said, "it is very uncomfortable to talk to someone who you feel has more information than you."

She nodded, and I left the room, carefully closing the door behind me.

The tanks had steamed up and drips of water ran down the sides of the glass, leaving trails in their wake. The sun had moved round to the window and shone through the vertical blinds, creating a pattern of horizontal stripes of light on the cream wall. I sat on the bed and looked at the boxes which I had yet to unpack. This was forty-two years of living: all the possessions I had gathered fitted into this one small room. This was the distillation of my life.

A piece of bacon had caught between my teeth and I could feel it with the end of my tongue; I reached into my mouth and attempted to remove it with a fingernail, but I couldn't quite get at it; I needed a toothpick, something sharp and thin enough to get between my teeth. There were some at home, in the bathroom, in the basket on the small cupboard.

At home. I had to stop this: this was now home. This room with its green walls, its painted fireplace and green carpet. Its single bed.

I thought I could feel the egg in my hand again; I felt its weight leave my palm and heard it smash on the floor. As before, my heart began to beat too quickly and I found myself experiencing a tightness in my head and my chest. I forced myself to slow my breathing. I held my head in my hands, recited to myself:

Dictyoptera is closely related to the orders of Orthoptera, Phasmida, Isoptera and Dermaptera.

All Pterygotes. The prefix *ptera*, meaning winged. As eqopposed to Apterygotes, the primitive, wingless insects whom evolution passed by.

The tightness in my chest remained. I lay back on the bed and forced my mind to be still, to focus. The compound eye, I told myself, is made up of ommatidia. Each ommatidium consists of the lens, a crystalline cone, visual cells, pigment cells. The composite of the responses of the ommatidia creates a mosaic image, and the quality of that image is dependent upon the number of ommatidia; the more numerous the images, the clearer the overall picture.

There was a quiet knock on the door and I heard Barbara's voice calling my name. I sat up and told her to come in.

She opened the door tentatively. "I thought I should make sure you're all right."

"I'm fine."

"Right. Good." She nodded towards the tanks. "They're okay?" she asked.

"They're fine too."

"They like it here, do they?"

"I think so," I said. "It's only their view of the outside world that has changed."

"Can they see out?"

"The glass steams up, with the humidity."

"Of course. D'you never tire of them?"

"I don't know how you could."

"Can I?" she said, gesturing to the closest of the tanks.

I nodded, and she walked over and stood for a long time looking at them. Then turned to me. "They are extraordinary."

I smiled. "I know." I got up and joined her. The female was absolutely still, her two legs in prayer. I lifted the lid of the tank and dropped in a small cricket. There was a flurry and then the cricket was struggling in her pincers.

"What happened?"

"Their movements are faster than our brains can register," I said.

We watched the mantid methodically consume the cricket, destroying it in her powerful, primitive mandibles.

"Does anything eat them?" she asked.

"Bats," I said. "In the wild they fly at night, you see. But they've learned to identify the sonar messages the bats send out, and they plummet to the ground when they hear them coming. They have an ear in their stomach.'

She shook her head. "Incredible."

"I know. They have extraordinarily highly developed survival skills."

She stepped back and saw the index card I had written and attached to the metal shelves.

Order – Dictyoptera.

Subgroup – Mantodea.

Families – Chaeteesidae; Metallycidae; Mantoididae; Amorphoscelidae; Eremiaphilidae; Hymenopodidae; Mantidae; Empusidae.

Most species are found within the Mantidae.

"What's this for?" she asked.

"I was teaching Tilly."

She smiled. "She's young for that."

I shrugged. "I knew it by her age."

She smiled again. "I'm sure you did."

We stood for a while, then she said my name. "Andrew, I just wanted to apologize." She ran her finger down the outside of the tank. "This is all really difficult, but I am trying my best."

"I know," I said.

"You see, I'm caught between you. It's just the territory we're in. But if I say or do anything to upset you, I want you to tell me."

I nodded. 'I'll try.'

"Good. What time do you drop the girls off?"

"Six or so."

"Where will you take them till then?"

"I don't know. I'll find somewhere."

"Make sure," she said, "that in amongst all this, you think of yourself."

"What do you mean?" I asked.

"Just that," she said. "Nothing more."

She took a last look in the tanks. "They're very beautiful," she said, "but they do frighten me."

Mantids and Other Dictyoptera

DIET

Although the mantid is renowned for its ability to catch its prey and consume it while still living, this act takes up only approximately 4% of its time. For 90% of its day the mantid is motionless, in a state of digestion, or pre-digestion. The remaining 6% is taken up with a combination of grooming and the changing of location.

By contrast, the live young are extremely active and disperse quickly from the ootheca, the egg case. In the first vulnerable period, they can become prey for ants and other predators; however, they soon gain their voracious appetite and learn their distinctive stillness, allowing their prey to approach them. If food is in short supply, the young mantids will consume their siblings. In captivity it is suggested that a large supply of live food (drosophila, other small flies) is provided to prevent cannibalism.

Adult mantids will consume crickets, waxworms, moths and butterflies. Large species will also consume small vertebrates, including tree frogs, mice, spiders, lizards and hummingbirds.

Mantids in captivity should be fed every alternate day with the following exceptions:

• Nymphs should have a constant supply of drosophila.
• Nymphs do not eat before and after moulting.

- Females should have extra food after laying an ootheca.
- Females should be well fed before mating to avoid cannibalism.

Andrew

Before I went to collect the girls from school, I drove out of the village and towards the sea. I wanted to be on my own for a while, but not in a bedroom with a single bed, and not in the town where I couldn't let myself into what had previously been my house.

I turned into a road I hadn't been down before. According to my map it was a dead end and stopped where the river entered the sea. The land either side was flat, with rough grasses and reed beds; the road itself was unsurfaced, and potholed, and I went as far as I could before parking and getting out. I climbed the gate and saw the stretch of sea to my left, the same grey as the sky, the horizon line slightly darker.

There were no houses in sight. Just the water ahead and the grass behind me: a bleak and elemental landscape. Gulls dropped, swooping from the sky, then returned to the clouds. The world of people and houses and the complications they brought with them felt so far away.

★

I drove back towards the town, slowing down as I passed the red-brick farmhouse. It was rundown, neglected. The gloss paint was chipped, and each window was shrouded in thick lace curtains. The barns and yard were disused.

I entered the town and parked. I walked to the school and waited by the gates. The first of the mothers emerged and passed me, a small child in hand. She smiled at me uncertainly, and hesitated, as if about to speak. I was going to say something when I thought I saw Tilly, so I stepped forward, but then saw there was a man next to her whom I didn't recognize. She was holding his hand. For a second I thought I must be mistaken, but she glanced in my direction and smiled, let go of his hand and ran to me.

The man called her name and she turned back. He held out her lunch box and book bag, and she took them from him. As he disappeared into the crowd of parents, I noted his closely cropped hair and ankle-length trousers, his sunglasses pushed to the top of his head, and the dark stain of tattooed letters running down one arm.

Tilly wrapped herself around my legs and looked up at me. "I didn't know you were coming."

"There must have been a mix-up," I said. I asked who the man was.

"Mum's friend," she said. "He's the man who sleeps in your bed."

I put my finger to my lips. "Shhh."

"But he is."

I grabbed her wrist and pulled her quickly towards the

gate. It was only when we got near Grace's school that I loosened my grip.

Tilly rubbed herself. "You hurt me," she said.

"I'm sorry," I said. "I didn't mean to. I was just in a hurry to get Grace."

The waitress hovered patiently with her small pad. Tilly snatched the menu from Grace's hand.

"Give us another minute, please," I said.

Grace turned from the window as the waitress left. "Why have we got to be here?"

I sighed. "You know why."

"The bird's at home waiting for food."

"I know," I said. "But if you go now I won't see you."

"But why've we got to sit here?"

"Where else could we go?"

Tilly put the menu down. "Why can't you just come home with us?"

I felt my heart start to quicken.

"Because he can't," Grace said.

"Why?"

"I don't live there any more," I said.

"But why?" Tilly asked. "Why?"

I caught the waitress's eye and she came over. Tilly asked for a portion of chips and a doughnut.

The waitress looked at me. "Separate plates?" she asked.

"I think so, don't you?" I glanced at Grace and smiled. "And tea for two," I said, "and a banana milkshake. You sure you don't want anything else, Grace?"

"No."

The waitress put her pen in her apron pocket and took the order to the kitchen. "You're letting her eat rubbish," Grace said.

"I don't want a scene."

"Because you feel bad about it all?"

I raised my hand to remonstrate with her, but at that moment, Tilly slipped out of her seat and under the table. I told her to sit up.

"The seat's slippy," she said.

"*Slippery*," I said. I looked over at Grace. "Are you all right?" She wouldn't meet my eyes, just shrugged.

"We talked about God today," Tilly said.

"Did you?" I asked. "What did you say?"

"I don't know who he is."

"You do," Grace said.

"I don't."

"You do God in reception class," Grace said. "So you must've done it."

"But I still don't know who he is."

The waitress returned with cups and saucers and a jug of milk. She placed a knife and fork wrapped in a paper napkin in front of Tilly, and then brought over a flaccid doughnut on a plate.

Tilly pulled it towards her; I pulled it back. "After the chips," I said.

Grace was looking out of the window again and I followed her gaze, to see what had caught her attention.

He was on the opposite side of the High Street, standing in a shop doorway, smoking, the tattoo showing. When he'd finished his cigarette, he flicked it into the gutter and walked off. I kept watching until I could see him no longer, then turned back. Grace and Tilly were both looking at me. I poured the tea.

Tilly ate her chips with her fingers, dipping them into the pool of ketchup on the side of the plate.

"Are you all right?" Grace asked.

"Absolutely fine," I said.

"You sure? You don't look it."

"I'm great," I said. "How are the chips?"

"Good," Tilly said, her mouth full. "Dad, did you know God wrote a book?"

"What book?" I asked.

"The Bibbel."

"Bible," I said.

She smiled. "That's it."

"It wasn't God who wrote it."

"It was. I know it was."

I started to correct her, but decided not to. I looked at Grace, who was staring out of the window again, both hands round her cup of tea, and remembered the egg in my hands, the cool shell, then the broken yellow and white mess on the floor. And I remembered the food in my mouth, the sensation of it blocking my windpipe.

I had to stop thinking like this, had to start thinking about the practical, the everyday things.

"Grace," I asked, "do you want more tea?"

She shook her head. "Dad," she said, "did I really save David's life?"

"No one will ever know for certain," I said. "But the chances are you did. He could have choked on his own vomit, lying like that."

"That's disgusting," Tilly said.

"A lot of people die that way," I said.

"I keep thinking about it," Grace said. "About if I hadn't gone for a walk that day. Do you think he would have tried again to—" She looked to see if Tilly was listening, then said, "You know, what he did. Would he have done it again?"

"He might have done. But even if he hadn't, he still could have died lying there, if no one had found him."

"But what if I had just gone to school? See, I keep thinking, there must have been a reason for me to go there."

"You think so?"

"Why else would it happen?"

"Because it did," I said. "Two things happened. One, for whatever reason he did what he did, and the rope broke and he fell. Two, you decided for some reason not to go to school. People fall from trees all the time and there's no one there to rescue them. People miss school all the time and there's no one for them to rescue."

She was silent for a while, considering.

"It's just the collision of the two things has confused you," I said. "Anyway, wasn't it the dog who found you and took you to him? If he hadn't had the dog, you'd never have found him."

"I suppose." She took one of Tilly's chips and ate it. "What about the bird, then?" she asked.

"That was a bit different."

"How?"

"You weren't supposed to be at school. And anyway, someone else could have rescued it. It wasn't in a wood away from anywhere."

"They wouldn't have looked after her like I did."

"No," I said. "That's true."

She was quiet for a while, then, "What was he like at school?"

"David?" I said. "He used to come into my room a lot. Helped me look after the insects. But I never really got to know him."

"Why did some of them hang round your room?"

I shrugged. "It was that or face the jungle outside."

She nodded.

"Grace. Why didn't you go to school that day?" She looked out of the window. "Grace?"

"I don't want to talk about it." She stood up. "Can we go?"

"Tilly hasn't finished."

"She can take it with her."

"Don't you want to spend this time with me?" I asked.

"Not like this, in a stupid cafe." Grace went into the toilet. A couple walking past outside caught my eyes, his hand in the back pocket of her jeans, her arm around his waist. How, I wondered, had this happened to us? How had we gone from having so much to this in such a short space of time? Our marriage was perhaps not entirely happy, but it had not been entirely unhappy either. It really felt that one moment we'd had a life, then the next moment we had this. This chaos.

"Dad."

I turned. Grace held Tilly by her hand. There was a small segment of doughnut on the plate, surrounded by sugar.

"Dad," Grace repeated.

"Yes."

"You keep drifting off," Grace said. "Are you all right?"

I took a breath. "Of course. I'm absolutely fine. Look, come on, it's time I got you back."

"You don't have to come with us," Grace said.

"I know, but I want to."

Tilly broke away from Grace and ran towards the door. Grace stopped her.

"Where are you going?" I asked.

Tilly shook her head. "Nowhere."

"What is it?"

Tilly looked down at the floor. "I don't want to go home," she said.

"It's all right," Grace said. "We'll see Dad tomorrow."

"Yes," I said. "You will."

When we reached the house, I stopped short of the front door. Tilly hugged me, her arms tight round my legs. Grace removed her key from her pocket, but before she could place it in the lock, the door opened and I saw the man from the playground. He stepped back and allowed the girls to enter, then looked at me and nodded.

He closed the door, the solid wood sounding heavy in the frame, the lock slotting deeply into the mechanism.

Rachel

I washed the vase and filled it with fresh water and the new, yellow tulips. I placed them on the table.

The front door opened and closed, and Dave came back into the kitchen, kissed me, and went out of the back door to the garden.

I dried my hands and wandered into the hall, put Grace's bag away, and picked up Tilly's lunch box. I looked in the living room. Grace was sprawled across the sofa, watching television. 'Hi,' I said. 'How was school?'

She shrugged.

'Where did you go with your father?'

'Why d'you want to know?'

'I just wondered,' I said. A movement outside caught my eyes and I lifted the net curtain. It was him, Andrew, standing there, staring at the house. I quickly stepped back. 'Grace. Why's your father there?'

'Why are you saying your *father*?' she asked. 'You didn't used to say that.'

'Don't ask difficult questions. What's he doing there?'

'I don't know, do I? He dropped us off.'

'I told you to come home alone.'

'I know what you told us,' she said. 'But he wanted to bring us.'

She turned up the volume of the television and I remained by the window, trying to watch Andrew without him seeing me. His hair was uncombed, due for a cut, his fringe falling on to his face. He wore shorts and his sandals, and a thin tee-shirt. He stood, unnaturally still, tense, arms at his sides, fists clenched.

I heard Dave call for me, then he appeared in the living-room doorway.

'What're you looking at?' he asked.

I turned from the window. 'Nothing.' I spoke quickly. 'Where did Tilly go?'

'Upstairs.'

Dave put his hand out to stop me. 'You gonna sit down, Rach? You've been on your feet all day.'

'I will in a second.' I pushed past him and climbed the stairs to Tilly's room.

I could see her through the open door, kneeling on the floor, her hair round her face, her back to me. The heels of her socks were discoloured, and I could just see her pants under her red-and-white checked dress. Her legs were still chubby, but she was beginning to stretch and develop a pre-adolescent body.

'Hi, Tilly,' I said. She looked round, then continued to play.

I edged past and saw she had her small bears in a pile, and had placed one of them in a small cardboard box, using a pile of tissues as blankets.

I looked out of the window, down at the road. Andrew was there still, in the same position, staring. As I watched, he rubbed his face, then turned and started walking away slowly, as though he couldn't bear to go.

Tilly had stopped playing and was watching me. 'What are you doing?'

I smiled. 'Nothing.'

'Is there something out there?'

I moved away from the window. 'No.'

She stood up and checked for herself. 'That was Dad.'

'He's just going,' I said.

'You didn't wave.'

'No,' I said.

'Why didn't you wave?'

I ignored her question and pointed to the bears on the floor. 'Are you making them all beds?' I asked.

She shook her head and was silent for a moment, then said, 'I don't like sleeping at Barbara's house. And I don't think Dad likes it.'

'Did he say that?'

'No, but I know what he likes.'

'Look,' I said quickly, crossing the room and picking up one of the bears, 'this one's cold. He needs tucking in.' I knelt down and began to fold the tissues.

She shook her head. 'You're too old to do that.'

'Am I?'

'Yes.' As she answered, I heard Dave's voice, calling my name up the stairs.

'I don't like him here,' Tilly said.

'I know,' I said. 'But I do.'

She shrugged. 'But I don't,' she said.

'Tilly,' I said. 'It makes me happy when he's here.' She said nothing. 'Don't you care if I'm happy or not?'

She shook her head. 'No.' She sounded surprised, as though the thought had never occurred to her.

I turned off the television and sat on the sofa, holding my tea. Grace had gone upstairs. Dave was in the kitchen, preparing food. The sun was disappearing from the front room now, inching its way round to the end of the street where it would later set.

I finished my tea and sat back, closed my eyes. It was difficult to rid my head of the image of Andrew standing there, outside the house, his fists clenched by his sides. His body had tightened since I met him, when he was loose-limbed, with a loping walk, eager to share his knowledge. That first day when I went into his classroom in error, and he showed me the tanks, he could have talked all morning, he said. When he talked about his extraordinary creatures, he would gesticulate passionately, creating shapes in the air in front of him.

From the day I brought him home with me, my father, normally so difficult to please, discussed him endlessly. He would give me books to give him, articles from his journals. And when he began to weaken and each breath cost him too much energy, he asked if I was going to spend my life with Andrew and I said yes, of course, and my father smiled and closed his eyes. Two days later, when my mother took him his early morning cup of tea, my father couldn't be woken.

Soon after eating, the girls went into the living room and turned the television on. Dave stood up from the table and got out another bottle of wine.

I placed my hand over my glass. 'I've had enough.'

'Just one,' he said. 'I can't drink alone.'

I moved my hand. 'A small one, then.'

He filled our glasses and raised his to touch mine. 'Cheers.'

'Cheers,' I said. 'You're a good cook.'

'I try.' He pressed his knees against mine, under the table. 'I know I have to go home tonight but I don't want to.'

'You're coming back tomorrow.'

He nodded. 'I know, but I still don't want to go.'

I smiled, then caught sight of us in the large mirror on the opposite wall. Seeing us together like that was a shock. His dark short hair and my dyed red hair, my lined face, my older self. I looked away quickly, had to stop questioning it: he'd told me he wanted to be with me; that should be enough.

'What are you thinking?' he asked.

'This and that.'

He smiled and leaned forward to kiss me.

'This and that?' he said.

'I was thinking of you.'

He smiled and we kissed again, and when I opened my eyes I could see Tilly standing in the doorway watching us.

The girls' bags were packed with their overnight things. I gave Grace her money, and handed Tilly her lunch box.

Grace was about to leave without saying anything, so I put my arm out to stop her. 'Aren't you going to kiss me goodbye?'

She shook her head and pushed me away.

'I'll kiss you,' Tilly said. She pursed her lips and I bent down to her.

'You know where to meet Daddy?' I asked.

She nodded. 'But I don't want to go there.'

'Don't be silly,' I said. 'You'll have a lovely time.'

'Who's going to be here when I'm not?' Tilly asked.

'Just me.'

Grace lifted her head and laughed. 'Oh yeh? Just you?'

'Don't make this difficult,' I said.

'Me make it difficult?'

'Yes, you.'

'You know what?' Grace said. 'You can't see anything any more, you've become so selfish.'

I stepped towards her. 'Don't speak to me like that.'

'Why? Why? Is it too honest? Too truthful?' She took Tilly's hand and pulled her out of the door. 'Come on.'

I watched until they disappeared round the corner at the end of the street, then I closed the door and sat on the bottom step of the stairs, giving myself a few moments to calm down before leaving for work.

Dave was waiting for me outside the clinic and we walked to the pub. He got the drinks and sat down. His tee-shirt sleeves were tight over his arms, the tattooed letters showing.

'I want to say thanks for everything,' he said, lifting his glass.

I picked up mine and sniffed. 'What is it?'

'Vodka.'

'I said I wasn't going to drink.'

'Come on, we're celebrating.'

'I've been drinking too much.'

He looked at me. 'Don't spoil it.'

'Okay,' I said. We touched glasses.

'You make me happy,' he said. 'Do I make you happy?'

'Of course you do.'

'Good. You know, Rachel, the girls will get used to it.' He drank, and I watched the muscles in his neck ripple as he swallowed. 'They'll have to. You've put other people first too much.'

I shrugged. 'I don't know.'

'Running around after Tilly, Grace telling you what to do.'

'Is that how it seems?'

'Yeh.' He reached over and took my hand. 'That is how it seems. But you're doing something about it. Putting yourself first.'

I took a sip. The vodka was strong, stronger than I had expected. Dave reached his leg out and I felt it slip behind mine, felt it entwine itself round me.

'Rachel,' he said, 'what was he like?'

'Who?'

'The man you married. Andrew.'

'I don't want to talk about him.'

'Why?'

I shook my head.

'Why?' he asked again. 'I need to know.'

'Why do you?' I asked.

'You were with him a long time. Did a lot together.'

'All that's in the past. Why does it matter?'

'I hate thinking about it.' He took both of my hands in his. 'Rachel, I'm sorry. I'm just being insecure. I'm sorry.'

'There's no need to be,' I said.

'No.' We sat in silence for a while, then he said, 'I think I just want you so much. You make me feel good.'

'Do I?'

He smiled and leaned forward over the table and kissed me. 'You do, yeh.'

We wandered home in the warm evening. His arm round my waist, his hand tucked into my back pocket. We went over the bridge, on to the path, and sat on the bench.

The river was low and the darkening sky was reflected in the water. He pulled me on to his lap and kissed me. 'Rachel,' he said. 'You have to tell me what he was like.'

'Not that again,' I said.

'Just tell me this once, and I'll stop asking.' He looked away. 'I know it's stupid of me, but I need to know.'

I shrugged. 'What is it you want to know?' His hand was on my thigh, and he moved it higher up. 'Stop,' I said.

'I can't.' He slipped his other hand under my top and the feel of him on my skin was hot and hard and I thought, Andrew would never have done that. He would have been crouched at the edge of the river, examining the grasses and the pattern of the flow of water.

He cupped my breast. Stroked my skin. 'He wasn't like this,' I said. 'He wouldn't have done this.'

'No?' He kissed my neck. 'Why not? Go on. Tell me. What was he like?'

'He was quiet,' I said.

'What kind of quiet?'

'A quiet kind of personality. An only child, like me. Very scientific.'

'What else?'

'I don't know what to say. I can't describe him in one sentence.'

'Try.'

'He wasn't what he appeared to be.'

'In what way?'

'It's hard to explain.' I went to stand but he grabbed my hand and stopped me. 'He was a real family man, but I suppose you could say he was detached. You know, not at the beginning, but later on.'

'What kind of detached?'

'It's hard to explain. He's fragile. Not physically. I mean mentally.'

'Is he interested in women?'

'No. He's interested in insects.'

He laughed. 'Insects?'

I tried to smile. 'Can we change the subject?'

'Just one more thing, then. What was he like in bed?'

I didn't answer for a second.

'Rachel?'

This time I did stand up. I turned to go, but he pulled me between his open legs, then closed them round me, held my hands so I couldn't move.

'Tell me.'

'Stop it.'

He shook me. Not hard. But it was enough. 'Tell me.'

'No.'

'You have to tell me.'

'Dave.' I said it louder. 'Dave. Let go.'

He did as he was told and released me. I stumbled and fell on to the grass. He jumped to his feet and reached a hand out but I didn't take it. I shook my head, looked down at the ground, my hair over my face.

'Rachel.' I felt his touch on my back. 'I'm sorry. I'm really sorry. It's my stupid insecurity. I want it to be just me and you.'

'Why?'

'I want you too much.'

'But I have children,' I said. 'Grace and Tilly.'

'I know, I know. I didn't mean that.'

'Didn't you?' I asked.

'No.' He took my hand. 'Come on, I'll take you home.'

Tilly

In the middle of the night if you wake up you can see things. You can see dark shapes in the room. If you don't like seeing the shapes, or they begin to move, you can close your eyes again.

If you close your eyes, you can still see things. You can see different-coloured lights. And if you really think about them, you can see people and animals. You can see insects.

In the attic room at Dad's new house the window was sloping, and there was no curtain. I could see stars, and I could see the moon which is far away and changes its shape.

I could hear Grace breathing. She didn't want to share a room with me. That's because she's older than me and thought I would make a mess.

I didn't make a mess. I can be tidy if I try.

My book was on my bed but I didn't need to look at the pages. If I think really hard I can see the pictures in my head. That night I could see Manty's face and her big eyes. And I could see the picture of her smiling when she looks at the little girl. That picture makes me hot inside.

I do know who God is. God is in charge of the world. He can change things and make weather. He can also make animals. I wish I could make animals. I would make small ones I could keep in my house.

I didn't want to be in that house.

I knew Dad was downstairs and if I really wanted to, I could have gone and seen him and got into bed with him.

I just wanted to be at home again.

Rachel

I woke in the middle of the night. The light from the street outside filtered through the lace curtain, making patterns in the silent room. I looked at Dave in bed next to me: the shape of his back, each short hair pushing out of his scalp. The silver chain around his neck, lying flat on his skin.

My mouth was dry and my heartbeat slightly fast. A feeling of unease. I had drunk too much, far too much. I needed water; I picked up the glass by my bed and went to drink, but it was empty.

I got out of bed carefully, but Dave must have sensed me, because he turned towards me, reached for me. I bent down and kissed his face, told him I was going downstairs.

I drank two glasses of water, then filled the glass again and carried it into the living room. My skirt and top were on the floor and I glanced at the wall, remembered standing there. Remembered coming back and drinking wine, then Dave saying the children are away, we can do anything. My belly contracted with a rush.

I stood where I'd stood last night. Tried to work out if

someone had passed, whether or not they'd have been able to see in. Whether we had thought to turn the light off so they wouldn't have seen us in the dark. The truth was, I had no recollection of turning the light off or of very much at all; the previous night was fragmented in my mind, and though I knew pieces of it might come back to me later, at that very moment they were missing.

I gathered the clothes from the floor and climbed the first flight of stairs, stopping because Tilly's door was open. The blind was up and yellow light from the street filled the room. She'd made the bed, and her clothes were in a neat pile on the chair. The small box remained on the floor, the smallest bear tucked up in tissue paper. I sat down on the edge of the bed. Tilly's nightdress was on her pillow, folded, and I touched it and put it on my lap, stroked it. She reminded me of my father, whose study was always so well organized, his files and books in alphabetical order; nothing was ever just placed somewhere. Tilly's books were in a stack on the bedside table, the top one with a bookmark tucked inside the front cover. She hadn't started it yet, and I knew it was because she would be reading her special book yet again. I put her nightdress on the pillow and went into Grace's room.

Two of Tilly's toy animals were on the floor where she must have been in there playing. There were clothes heaped on the chair, and the bed was unmade. On the mantelpiece there were open pots of make-up which I lifted up and sniffed. The smell reminded me of being the same age, those first exhilarating occasions when I went out in the evenings, when my father would wait up, ready to cross-question me, his disapproval only too obvious. If he could see me now, here in this house with another man, Andrew standing outside watching.

I straightened the duvet and pillows, then sat down to fold her nightdress.

It was only happiness I wanted, something for me. I had spent too many years waiting, waiting for my time again, but also waiting on other people. My life had been pushed aside, placed on hold for too long. And anyway, it wasn't as if I was asking for something no one else had.

The door opened, brushing over the thick carpet and letting light from the landing fall into the room in a widening arc. Dave leaned in the doorway, wrapped in a towel again, tight round his body.

'What are you doing?' he asked.

'Nothing,' I said. 'I was just thinking. I couldn't sleep.'

He walked over to the window and peered out, then moved to stand by the fireplace. He looked at my reflection in the mirror, spoke to that rather than me. 'What is it?'

'Nothing,' I said to the mirror.

'What were you thinking about?'

I shook my head.

He turned and came over to me, the real me. He bent and lifted my chin so I had to meet his gaze. 'You seem so sad. What is it?'

'I was just thinking,' I said.

'What? Tell me. What were you thinking about?'

'My dad.'

He slipped his arm round my shoulder, then sat beside me.

'You poor little thing,' he said. He rested his hand on my thigh. 'Does it upset you to think of him?'

'A bit,' I said.

'We'll have to cheer you up.'

His hand crept higher and he pushed me back on to the bed. I shoved him away.

'What? What is it?'

'Not here,' I said. 'Not on her bed.'

'She won't know.'

'No,' I said. 'But I will.'

He sighed. 'Come on, then. Back to our bed.'

My hand in his, I followed him out of the room and up the stairs. I tried to ignore it, but there was a feeling of unease deep down inside my belly.

When I woke again, the sun had risen. Dave was leaning on one elbow, looking down at me.

I blinked, rubbed my eyes. My head was thick, heavy and my mouth tasted foul. I checked the clock: less than two hours till I had to leave for work.

Dave went to get some water and make tea, then sat on the side of the bed and watched me drink. My legs felt trapped by his weight dragging down on the covers. I turned to put the glass down but he took it from me. 'How are you?'

'I feel terrible,' I said.

He took my hand and rubbed it. Leaned forward and kissed me.

I shook my head. 'Don't.'

He held my hand, tightly. Leaned forward and stroked my hair. I pushed him away.

'You're heavy,' I said. 'I can't move.'

He stood up but didn't move away. He stood by the bed and looked at me.

His eyes always on me. Watching.

'I need a bath.' I got out of bed and left the room.

I lay in the hot bath water, my hair floating, weightless. I lifted one foot up and rested my big toe on the tap and closed my eyes. I wondered what he would think if he could see me now, the man I had been married to. Was still married to.

I rubbed the shampoo into my hair, conscious of the shape of my skull under my hands. The silence in the house was odd, uncomfortable, as though I'd had a radio on for fifteen years, and someone had turned it off. This endless thing that is having children, years of waking and getting them up, of running after them, repeating the same instructions over and over. Reading that same book at bedtime. Every word the same.

And all that time your own life and desires and wishes, on hold.

I leaned back and the shampoo clouded the clear water. I closed my eyes and dunked my head right under, running my hands through my hair. My ears were beneath the surface and I could hear the muffled sounds of the water lapping at the edge of the bath, could feel it against my face.

It was time to be definite. I couldn't afford to lose hours, to have memories of evening and nights fragment. I would not drink. I would not touch any alcohol until the weekend. Andrew hadn't ever got quite so drunk, not to forget what had happened.

I thought of the moment I had told him it was over, and he would have to find somewhere to go. That I would stay here, as the girls needed somewhere secure and stable to live. His eyes, blinking. His hand reaching out to me, featherlight fingers.

My eyes still closed, I lifted my head, my hair heavy. I squeezed off the excess water and opened my eyes.

Dave stood by the bath, looking down at me. I wrapped my arms around me, sat further forward to cover myself up.

He frowned. 'Don't do that.'

'I'm getting out,' I said.

'Lie back, like you were. I want to look at you.'

'I've got things to do,' I said. 'I have to go to work.'

He placed his hands on my shoulders and pushed gently and I let him. I lay back in the bath and he stood and looked at me for a long time till I thought he must be able to see what was inside me, till he could see the blood through my veins, the swelling and contraction of my lungs, the beating of my heart.

★

I pressed the cafetière plunger down. Glanced at Dave, sitting at the table, silent, staring out of the window.

'Why so quiet?' I asked.

He shrugged. I poured the coffee into the mugs, carried them over.

'What is it?' I asked.

He shook his head. 'Nothing.'

'Is it something I said? Something I've done?'

'No.'

'What then?'

'What are you doing today?' he asked.

'I have to go to work. You know I do.'

He placed his cup down, put both hands on the table and laced his fingers together.

'Come on. What is it?' I asked.

'I don't want to worry you,' he said. 'I can sort it.'

'Sort what?'

'It's just—' He hesitated, then started again. 'Just I have to find somewhere to live. I've been asked to move out.'

I sipped my coffee. 'I thought you were going to tell me something terrible.'

'It is terrible. I've got to my age and I don't even have my own house.'

We sat in silence for a while, then I stood up, fetched the coffee and milk, refilled his mug.

'Rachel,' he said, 'is there any way I could come and stay?' I opened my mouth to explain that under the circumstances it might be too soon, but before I could say anything, he spoke again, quickly. 'Just till I get something else.'

'I don't know,' I said. 'Andrew only moved out recently.'

'It would only be a few days. I don't know what else to do.'

'Do you not have anywhere else to stay?'

'Not really, no.'

'Then I suppose you'll have to come here,' I said.

'Oh, Rach. Thank you.'

He drained his coffee, then put his mug down. 'Thank you,' he said again. 'I'm really grateful.'

'It's okay,' I said. 'You don't have to keep saying it.'

That afternoon I left work five minutes late and had to run to the school. By the time I got to the gates most of the children were already out, and I rushed into the playground. Andrew was standing there, Tilly with him. They didn't see me and I stood watching, catching my breath for a second before approaching.

'Andrew,' I said. 'What are you doing here?'

He looked at me, startled. 'I came to get Tilly.'

'It's Thursday,' I said. 'She comes home with me.'

'Does she?'

'You know she does.' I took Tilly's lunch box from him. 'What are you doing?'

He stared at me. 'I don't know.'

I reached for Tilly's hand but she slipped away and hugged Andrew's legs. 'Come on, Tilly,' I said, 'we have to go.' I unpicked her fingers and pulled her towards me. She started to cry.

'You see what you've done, Andrew,' I said. 'You have to stick to the agreement.' I took Tilly's hand in mine and dragged her out of the playground.

Early that evening I stood at the kitchen sink and peeled the potatoes. The sink was full of scrapings and cold water, the water was discoloured from the mud. My hands felt numb and the potatoes slimy and I didn't want to eat them anyway. I threw the peeler into the water and wiped my hands.

Grace sat at the table, her books open and her pen in her mouth. She stared out of the window.

'Where's Tilly?' I asked. Grace didn't move, just sat there staring. 'Grace, where's Tilly?'

Before she could answer, the doorbell rang. 'You getting that?' I asked.

She shook her head. 'It'll be him.'

'Don't be like that,' I said, walking into the hall.

I could see the shape of him through the patterned glass, a kaleidoscope of shapes and colours, his image divided and fragmented.

I opened the door and saw he had a couple of bags with him. I pointed at their bags. 'What are those?'

'My stuff. I said I'd get the rest at the weekend.'

'Oh.'

'What?' he asked. 'What is it?'

'Nothing. I just didn't know it'd be that soon.'

'I thought it was okay. You said it was.'

'I know I did. But I haven't said anything to the girls.'

I stood aside to let him in and followed him along the hall and into the kitchen.

I watched Grace notice the bags, saw her lift her head and narrow her eyes. 'What are those?'

'Dave's come to stay for a bit,' I said. 'He's been thrown out of his place.'

There was a long silence.

'I'll take these up,' Dave said, and left the room.

I took some knives and forks out of the drawer and counted them. Four of each. Grace was staring at me. Eventually I spoke. 'What?'

'Why didn't you tell us?'

'I was going to.'

'But you didn't.'

I sighed. 'It was all a bit last minute.'

'I don't want him here.'

I slammed the knives and forks on the table. 'I know you don't.'

'Dad's only just gone.'

'Look,' I said, 'I'm not answerable to you.'

'No,' she said, 'I know. You're not answerable to anyone any more.'

'Grace, I'm a human being,' I said. 'What do you want from me? That I join a fucking nunnery? Would that make you happy? Would it?'

She didn't flinch. Just closed her school books. 'Have you finished?' she asked. Slowly. Calmly.

I said nothing. She got up and left the room.

'Grace,' I called. 'Grace. Come back.' But she'd gone.

I stood by the sink and looked down at the cold, wet potatoes in the dirty water. My desire to walk out of the kitchen and out of the door was overwhelming. Just to walk and walk out of my own life and never look back. I held on to the edge of the sink as though it would keep me there.

Grace

I could feel the quick beat of the bird's heart where her throat was resting between my first finger and thumb. Her skin was paper-thin, and among the soft yellow feathers there were hard adult feathers piercing through. Her beak was still far too big for her, but she was starting to look less ugly.

When David was in the hospital, and I sat and watched him sleep, I had seen a tiny pulse in his neck. And in the woods when I found him, when he lay in the moss and leaves, I had seen a pulse in the lid of his closed eye.

I was thinking about him more and more. The pale eyes and the red in his hair.

I got the tea towel and wrapped the bird in it and held her on my lap. I took a small pellet of wet brown bread and went to lever her beak open, but for the first time, she needed no help. I pushed the bread to the back of her tongue and she swallowed.

The door opened. Tilly stood in her nightdress and waited for me to tell her to go back to bed. When I didn't say anything she came into the room and knelt in front of me, stroking the bird's head with her finger.

—You like her? I asked.

—I love her.

I laughed. —You love everything, Til.

—Will she fly when she's older? she asked.

—Probably, I said. —That's what birds do.

She smiled. —I know. I'm not stupid.

—I know you're not stupid, I said. —I was teasing. We'll have to let her go. That's why I'm trying not to touch her too much. She has to go back to the wild.

—Is that why she hasn't got a name?

—Yes, I said. I unwrapped the bird and returned her to the cage that Dad had made for me. She walked up and down and stretched her wings.

—I don't want her to go.

—No, I said. —I know, but she has to.

I put the cage on the shelf, then looked back at Tilly sitting on the floor. —What are you doing up anyway? I asked. —You should be in bed.

Tilly put her hands over her ears. —I can't hear you.

I ran over and tickled her. —You can.

—I can't.

—You heard me then. Or you wouldn't have said can't.

—Oh, she said. —Grace, can I sleep in here with you?

—Why? I asked. —What is it?

—Why's Mum gone out with that man? I want him to go home. I don't want him staying here. I want Dad back.

—I know you do, I said. I felt a weight inside me, dropping down.

—Do you think he's going to come back? she asked.

I looked at the window. —I don't know, Til. I don't know what to say to you.

—Well, he won't come back while that man's here, she said.

—No, I said. —You can be very grown-up sometimes.

—I am six, she said. She caught me laughing. —Don't laugh at me.

—No, I said. She stood up and I caught sight of something silver in her hand. I made her show me. It was a crumpled piece of silver foil.

—It was an animal, she said. —See.

She took the foil and pulled out the corners.

—It has four legs and a tail and a head. I've got lots upstairs. I made it myself.

—I guessed that, I said.

—The teacher read us a book at school, she said. —I don't know what it was called, but the girl in it had toy animals and they became real.

I nodded. —And do you think these will?

She looked at me carefully. —Do you think they will?

—I don't know. Maybe when you're asleep they will.

—Maybe, yes.

She was quiet for a while, thinking, I knew, of the foil animals coming to life, beginning to walk.

—I'm going to make some more, she said. —I want to make an insect. Are insects animals?

—They're part of the animal kingdom.

—Dad told me they have different bits to their bodies. There's over a million different ones.

—Til, I said, —we can't stay here and talk about insects all night. It's late. Come on. Up to bed.

—Where's Mum?

—You know where she is, I said. —They'll be back later.

—I don't want him to come back. She started to cry. —I want my dad.

—No, don't cry, Til. I opened my arms. She reached for me and I picked her up and put her in my bed. I held her till she fell asleep, then I went downstairs and made a drink, which I took into the living room.

I sat in the chair with my knees drawn close to my chest. Soft yellow light came in from outside and there were shadow patterns on the wall from the lace curtains.

The books on the shelves stretched from ceiling to floor. Science, nature, animals and birds. They were my grandfather's books, and Dad used them all the time. I saw him looking at them the day he packed, running his hand along them, touching their spines.

It felt like everything in the house had changed.

I closed my eyes and rested my head on the back of the chair. Too much had happened. I thought of the morning after Dad took his things, and David's face as he lay in the leaves. And his face in the frame, surrounded by words. *Kiss the son lest he be angry.*

I heard laughing from the street, then the key in the door, their voices in the hall.

—Come on, love.

—No. Stop it. What about the girls?

—They're asleep. Come on.

—Dave. Don't.

I grabbed a book from the table and dropped it on the floor. The voices stopped, then I heard her. —What's that?

—Nothing, he said.

The living-room door opened and the light went on. She saw me sitting there and looked at me for a moment. Then she spoke.

—You okay, Grace?

I said nothing.

—Grace, I said you okay?

I stood up and brushed past her. I kept my eyes to the floor so I didn't have to see them. Dave was standing there at the bottom of the stairs and I made sure not to touch him as I walked by. He ran up after me though and caught my arm. He checked Mum couldn't hear, then said, — Spying, are we?

I shook his hand off and escaped to my room.

Tilly was sprawled across the bed; I thought about carrying her to her room, but she put her arms around my neck and pulled me down to her. I shifted her over towards the wall, then turned out the light and got in beside her.

The Unhappy Insect

One day Manty heard the door to the room open and she waited for the lid to go up and for the hairy hand to throw in more food.

Dead food.

She felt so sad. Poor, poor Manty.

But then she saw something move in the room. She thought she could see something red. It looked like a red dress. And then she heard a voice. It sounded like a young girl's voice.

Manty was confused. What on earth could be happening? Then the lid of the tank was lifted off and Manty saw a young girl looking in.

'Hello,' the girl said. 'You look sad. I'm going to take you home with me.'

Manty looked up from the dead branch and saw the girl smiling. Manty smiled too. The two of them smiled at each other.

Grace

The following morning I took Tilly to school. I left her at the gate, then looked up towards my school, before turning my back on it and walking in the other direction past the shops, out through the edge of the town, to where the houses ended and the fields began.

I walked along the top of the river bank, following the flow of the water. The reeds moved just under the surface, dirty green ribbons swaying from side to side.

When I reached the farmhouse, I crossed the yard. Clumps of moss grew on the grey ribbed concrete, and there was an open sack of cement which had hardened, a rusted trough.

The big barn doors were open and I stepped inside. The air was dry and the floor littered with piles of bird droppings. At one end there was a pile of gates and at the other bales of stale hay which had come undone.

I breathed in and smelled the air. My body felt tired and I curled up on the hay, closed my eyes.

There was a light wind outside and I could hear it

rustling the leaves of the trees that bordered the yard. I thought I could hear the river too, rippling and swirling towards the sea, pulled by the moon and tides. The soft soil of the banks would be crumbling and falling into the water, pieces sinking down into the dark. Below, the fishes would be swimming, their scales sliding over each other, their gills opening and closing.

Perhaps a silver eel would be slipping through the grass, down the side of the bank, into the thick red-brown water.

No one knew where I was.

No one.

I woke to the sounds of the wind outside, and the pigeons above. I sat up and picked the strands of hay off my clothes.

I left the barn and walked around the outside of the house, to the back door. The handle opened. I walked through the scullery into the kitchen. The table had two plates on it and a loaf of bread. A teapot under a woollen knitted teapot cover, and two cups. A jug with a small net over it, weighted down by glass beads.

The frame was still on the wall, the words bordering the photograph. *Kiss the son lest he be angry.* I read the words wrapped round the doorway that led into the hall: *I will offer unto thee burnt sacrifices of fatlings, with the incense of rams; I will offer bullocks with goats.*

I passed the phone I had used that day to ring for the ambulance, and went up the stairs. In the centre of each step there was a thin strip of carpet held in place by brass rods and the landing floorboards were bare. The doors to the rooms were the same dark, brittle varnish as down-stairs.

The bathroom door was ajar and I could see the black lino and a mint-green bath with high silver taps, stained with limescale. The window was slightly open, and the free end of a roll of toilet paper on the windowsill fluttered in the breeze.

In the next room there was a large red patterned rug on stained floorboards. Thick red curtains hung on metal tracks. Against the wall there was a high iron bed. Above the bed a tapestry in a wooden frame. *God has time to listen if you have time to pray.*

There was one other room. Floorboards again, and a green rug. A large, dark wardrobe and boarded-up fireplace. A single bed. A blue tee-shirt on the chair. David's room.

On the table by the window I could see a tank, similar to Dad's, the glass streaked with condensation. I was about to take the lid off to look inside when I heard something on the stairs. I backed against the wall as David opened the door.

—What are you doing here?

—I'm sorry, I said. —I'll go home. I moved towards the door.

He stood in my way and put out his hand to stop me. —I asked you what you were doing here.

I shook my head. —I don't know.

As I spoke, the sun emerged from behind the clouds and shone into the room, lighting up the colours in his hair. He hadn't shaved and his beard stubble was a mix of red and blond. The bruises on his neck had faded and I could hardly see them.

—I came to see you, I said. —I wanted to see the house again.

He nodded, then walked to the open window and looked out. I looked out from behind him and we could see the length of the garden, along the concrete path, to the willow and the river beyond. I imagined the tree at the end of the garden bending over, the ends of its long branches and its leaves trailing on the surface of the river, being drawn one way by the current, held back by the roots of the tree.

There was the sound of a car in the yard and he moved quickly to the door. I followed him.

His mother entered the kitchen, wearing a faded apron on top of her clothes, and her knitted hat. She put a bag on the chair and looked at me.

—It's Grace, David said. —She's come to see us.

His mother gestured for me to pull out a chair and sit down. We stayed like that for a while. David in front of the window. His mother on the chair opposite me, her hat crushing her grey hair. Then, —Your name is Grace, she said.

I nodded. —Yes.

—He told you to go there.

—Who? I asked.

—He knows what He is doing. This is all part of His pattern which we have to learn to read.

There was a silence. The three of us in that room with the sun and the river flowing past at the end of the garden. I went to stand up. —I need to go, I said. —I have to get home.

—You'll come back, his mother said.

It wasn't a question, but I answered anyway. —I don't know.

—You will, she said.

Thou visitest the earth, and waterest it: thou greatly enrichest it
with the river of God, which is full of water: thou preparest
them corn, when thou hast so provided for it.

Thou waterest the ridges thereof abundantly: thou settlest
the furrows thereof: thou makest it soft with showers:
thou blessest the springing thereof.

Thou crownest the year with thy goodness; and thy paths
drop fatness.

They drop upon the pastures of the wilderness:
and the little hills rejoice on every side.

The pastures are clothed with flocks; the valleys also are
covered over with corn; they shout for joy, they also sing.

At home, I closed the door carefully behind me and stood in the hall. I lifted my hand to my face and breathed in the smells I'd brought back with me. The hay and dust of the barn. The air outside. The silence.

The house was quiet and I went into the kitchen. On the table was a newspaper, and next to that, a pack of cigarettes and a heavy gold lighter. Dave's. One of Dad's water sprayers lay on the windowsill, where he must have left it by mistake. Seeing it, I thought of his thin body standing over the insects, leaning forward slightly, lost in the damp soil and humid air, the mantids' prayers.

And David, in his room, his tank with the steamed-up glass.

I picked up Dave's cigarettes and took them out one by one. I ripped the thin paper and let the dry strands of tobacco fall on to the table, then crumpled the empty packet in my hand and flicked open the lighter and held it to the cardboard until the flame caught and I felt the heat on my fingers. As it burned, I dropped it on to the floor and stamped on it.

I closed my eyes and let myself imagine sinking back down into the hay, thinking of the river and the fish moving below. The silver eel on the green of the grass.

A loud noise made me jump. I stood still. I could hear feet coming down the stairs, then along the hall. There was a creak, then the handle turned and the door into the kitchen opened.

Mum looked at me, then walked over and saw the mess on the floor and table.

—What have you done? Grace?

I swept the tobacco strands and cigarette husks into my hand and put them into the bin. —Nothing, I said. —I was just playing around.

—Just playing around? And I suppose it just happened to be his cigarettes? I heard her take a deep breath. —You're beginning to make this really difficult. You know that?

I refused to meet her gaze.

—Have you thought about me, about how you being difficult makes me feel? She waited. —Have you?

I said nothing.

—Look, she said. She waited, and I knew she was trying to calm down, get her voice to sound reasonable. To deal with her difficult daughter. —Look, she said again, —you have to see it from my point of view. Your father and I have separated. What am I supposed to do? Spend the rest of my life on my own?

I stared at her bare feet. The chipped blue varnish had gone and her nails were painted pink. I thought about what she had asked me. *Did* I expect her to spend the rest of her life alone? For a second I thought it was me, that I was acting unreasonably. But I thought about how quickly everything had changed. It was too early for any of this. I wasn't asking her to be alone for ever.

—Grace?

—I don't know, I said.

—Well, think about it. Unless you want me unhappy. Do you? Maybe that's what you want.

I shook my head. It wasn't that. But was this the only way she could be happy? What about us? Dad, Tilly, me? I felt tied up, caught in her sentences. Whatever I said she would twist it, bring it back to the accusation that I wanted her to be single, unhappy.

—Where have you been anyway? she asked.

I walked over to the window.

—You've been somewhere. You've got dry grass on you.

I could see the garden, and the climbing frame. I could see the reflection of her shape behind me. The outside and the inside at the same time.

—Grace. I'm talking to you. I asked you where you've been. The school rang me. I had to leave work, but I couldn't find you anywhere. I've been here waiting. Grace?

I said nothing. I didn't want to tell her. It was mine, something no one else knew about.

She stepped towards me. —Why're you covered in hay? She grabbed my shoulders and turned me around to face her. —It's time you told me where you've been going. Grace?

—I went to see David, I said. —The man I found in the woods.

—Why?

—I don't know.

—What's he want with a young girl like you?

—It's not like that, I said.

She laughed. —No?

I stared at her. —No, I said. —It isn't.

—You must think I'm stupid, she said. —You've been off with him.

—Is that what you think? I asked.

—That's exactly what I think, she said. —He's not exactly stable, this man you found. He takes himself off into the woods, tries to kill himself. I mean, why did he do that? Why?

—I haven't asked him.

—So you didn't ask and he didn't think to mention it.

—No.

—How can you be so stupid?

She still had hold of my shoulders and now she shook me. I allowed her to, although I wanted to shove her right away, leave me alone.

—I don't want you going there again, she said. —You hear me? Never.

A small voice inside me spoke. Let her think what she wants to think, and she'll leave you alone.

—I heard you, I said.

She nodded, and released me.

The teacher's door was slightly open and I knocked on it.

He sat behind the desk and pointed at the chair opposite. He threaded his fingers through each other.

He smiled at me. —Why do you think I've asked

you to come and see me? He unthreaded his hands and leaned forward. —Grace. We know things aren't good for you.

I looked down at my lap. Couldn't bear his voice, the way it tried to get right inside me and find everything out.

—Grace. We can't allow you to keep disappearing. We can't pretend it's not happening. We have a duty of care towards you.

The word *care* hit somewhere deep down. I bit my bottom lip and made myself think of standing in the barn. The call of the pigeons. The smell of the hay.

—There may be something we can do for you.

I shook my head.

—Nothing we can help with?

I tried to say no but when I opened my mouth it wouldn't come out. He took a tissue from the box and passed it to me.

—Where is it you go when you don't come here?

I held the tissue tight in my hand. —I go walking.

—Where do you walk?

—Everywhere, I said.

I walk to my secret place and no one knows where I am. It is mine and when I am there I am me.

—Grace. He waited till I looked up at him. —How is your dad?

I shrugged.

—He did tell me what happened, you know, with your mum.

I still kept looking at my lap, my hands. If he knew that,

he must know how my dad was. Another adult asking a question they already knew the answer to. I tightened my fingers around the tissue.

—It's not going to be an easy time for you, he said. — It isn't for anyone going through this. But we'll be here, and you can come and see me whenever you want. Just try and stay at school. It will get better.

Better? It will get better? I should have asked how, should have said, tell me exactly how it's going to get better. But I didn't. Couldn't speak. So I nodded, not because I agreed, but to make *him* feel better, and I stood up and left the room.

I walked down the corridor to my classroom. Through the glass panel in the door, I could see my bag resting on the floor by my chair. I saw the teacher at the front, by the board. I saw the others in their chairs. If I went in and sat down they would all look at me. Look through me. See what was inside me.

I couldn't do it.

I turned and walked back down the corridor, out on to the playing field, through the gap in the hedge.

It was dark inside, and much cooler than outside. I looked around at the empty seats and then up at the high ceiling. I read the noticeboard with its list of names for flower and brass cleaning duty, one for each week. And the poster announcing a lunch, a bowl of lentil soup and a chunk of bread, in exchange for a donation to a programme in Africa. And next to that a photograph of a man wearing a black and white collar, with a group of young children, their skin purple-black in the strong sunlight.

On the table in front of the noticeboard there was a book. In the columns, people had written the date, their name and home town, then comments. I read the last entry, an address in Yorkshire. *Looking for my mother's family. Thank you for the quiet moment.* The entry before that was in small, tidy writing. An address in London. *Another of God's houses.*

I flicked through the book. The earlier entries were faded and the pages were worn. There were only ten comments from this year.

At the far end of the church, a table covered in a cloth, the name of the church embroidered on it and weighted down by two heavy brass candlesticks. Either side were wooden seats, smooth from years of use. I sat in one. There was a Bible in front of me and I picked it up. It was open at Psalm 51. *I know all the fowls of the mountains: and the wild beasts of the field are mine.* And below that were the words I had seen before. *Will I eat the flesh of bulls, or drink the blood of goats?*

The church door banged shut behind me as I walked out on to the short green grass, into the sun.

I heard a car and stepped on to the verge, halfway up the river bank. The car slowed and stopped. Dad leaned across the seat, opened the passenger door, and I climbed in.

He drove in silence, right out through the fields, past his village and along a small lane bordered by reed beds.

Then the road ended and he parked. I could see the grey-brown water where the river spilled out into the sea. There were no houses. No people. Just the water and sky.

We sat there for a while, then eventually I spoke. —Dad, I said, —what's going to happen?

He didn't answer for a bit and I wondered if he'd heard me. Or if I'd even said the words.

Then he sighed. —I don't know.

—That man has moved in. He says he was thrown out of where he lives and had nowhere else to go. I don't want him there. Tilly doesn't either.

There was a long pause.

—I don't know what I can do.

—Will you talk to her?

He shook his head slowly.

—You have to try, I said. —Someone has to talk to her.

—She won't talk to me.

—I don't want to go back home, I said. —I don't want to go to school either.

—You have to go to school.

—Dad, I said, —can we get my bird from Mum's and go back to your house? You wouldn't have to go in or anything, I'd be really quick.

—It's not my turn to have you, he said.

—But what about what I want?

—Grace. He paused again, then spoke carefully. —I'm scared if I don't do what I'm told I may not be able to see you.

I sat and thought about what he said for a while. It hadn't ever occurred to me he wouldn't be able to see me and I didn't really understand what he meant. He was my father, my dad.

I looked at him, his arms resting on the steering wheel, his head on his arms. His thin legs and pale skin.

—Dad, I said.

—What?

—Are you all right?

He nodded without lifting his head.

—You look so thin, I said. —Have you been eating?

—You're not to worry about me, he said. —You understand? I don't want that. I'm fine.

—Okay.

We sat there for a while, surrounded by the water and the sky.

—I come here a lot, he said.

—Why?

He looked out over the landscape. —Because there's no one here. No houses. Just this. This and the birds. It's all simpler here. Pure. I feel easier here.

I thought of the barn, the nest of hay, where I felt easier, simpler, purer.

—Dad, I said, —I went to David's house and he had a tank there.

He smiled. —I gave him a tank once, an old one we had in the lab. I wonder if it's the same one. What's he keeping?

—I don't know. I didn't see.

—I keep remembering more about him. He used to come and help me a lot. Hardly spoke, just used to watch them and help feed and clean them. How is he?

—He's better.

—Good.

I opened the car door. The air was still. Warm. Dad followed me and we walked to the edge of the grass and looked over the stretch of water, then went back to the car and he drove me to the town, took me home.

I closed my bedroom door and took the bird out. She sat on my lap and opened her beak for her food. I tried not to touch her, tried not to allow myself to get close to her, but I did allow myself to stroke the new feathers on the top of her head and pick off the hard shell coating. She closed her eyes and tipped her head towards me.

I put her back into her cage and she watched me through the bars as I picked up my pen and began writing on the wall.

I drew the outline of a large K, then continued. *Kiss the son lest he be angry.*

I used the pots of make-up from the mantelpiece and a fine brush and began filling in the K with red and gold. When I had finished I sat on my bed and looked at it.

There was a knock on the door. Mum entered.

—What the hell are you doing? she asked, her voice sharp. —You realize no one was there to get Tilly? Anything could have happened.

I glanced at her but said nothing. I didn't have to speak. She couldn't make me.

She gazed around the room. —What's going on?

Then she saw the wall. She stared at it for a moment, then turned to me.

—It's him, isn't it? You've been there again. You have.

I went to the window, stood with my back to her.

—The school called me in. I had to sit there and listen to how many days you've missed. It has to stop, you hear? Grace. Do you hear me?

I wanted to stop her, wanted to place my hand over her mouth and muffle her voice.

—I said it has to stop. Tell me you won't go to see him any more.

Tell me, tell me. Muffle her voice till she stopped and left me alone.

—Grace, Mum shouted, —I told you to stop going down there. What's he want with you anyway?

I still said nothing.

—You know what you are, don't you? You're like a bitch on heat.

I stopped breathing and spun round to look at her.

In my mind, a voice. Words. *Deliver my soul from the sword; my darling from the power of the dog.*

She shook her head, took a tiny step towards me. —I didn't mean that.

—You did, I said. —That's what you think of me.

—No.

138

—It's too late. You said it. You said it and you won't ever be able to take it back.

She stood, shaking her head, and I opened the door.

—I want you to go now.

I shut the door behind her and went back to the window. And then I saw Dad in his car, sitting there, looking at the house, even though it had been hours since he dropped me off.

Mantids and Other Dictyoptera

MYTHOLOGY AND FOLKLORE

'The mantis is not strong enough to stop the bullock cart, but is brave enough to try.'

Throughout history, we see the mantid appear in folklore and mythology. This is perhaps because of its distinctive posture, but also because of its cannibalistic nature and highly developed survival skills.

Beliefs common across different cultures include the mantid forecasting changes in the seasons and having the ability to direct lost and missing persons. There is one recurring belief, though the details may change according to time and place, which is that the mantid has particular religious or spiritual powers. The word mantis derives from the Greek *mantes* for prophet, and myths include the mantid praying towards Mecca (which obviously incorporates elements of the mantid understanding directions), and worshipping the Christian God.

Specific examples from folklore include the following:

In African villages, a mantis is thought to be an incarnation of the witch doctor from the neighbouring village, spying on the community. The mantid is also believed to have the ability to restore life if it lands upon the corpse of a human being.

DEVOTION

In France, a lost child is urged to find a mantis, who will then point the way home.

In China, the mantid is frequently associated with bed-wetting. It is a common belief that feeding roasted egg cases (ootheca) to children will help prevent bed-wetting.

In the United States of America, the brown saliva of the mantid can kill a horse, its poison is so powerful.

'The mantid seizes the locust, but does not see the yellow bird behind him.'

Andrew

I closed the book and looked across the landscape: the grey sea, grey sky. If I could only lose myself in the water, float away on it until I hit that grey line of horizon. I would melt into it and become greyer and greyer until I disappeared. I put the book on the passenger seat and leaned my head on the headrest and closed my eyes.

I'd been there since dawn, had not been able to remain a moment longer in the house without the girls. I had begun to ache for them, physically ache. The days had no rhythm without them to wake, feed, take to school, help with homework. I didn't know what to do any more. The hours rolled out in front of me, empty and senseless; nights were the same, only dark.

In my attempt to make sense of all that had happened, sentences chattered in my mind: phrases of discussions with Rachel, old arguments, new silences and misunderstandings. Questions too: why now? why him? why in our house? It was becoming an endless loop of noise in my head. A chaotic symphony.

As I stared at the sky and sea, they seemed to part, and the horizon widened, a long grey crack. A yellow stain appeared and dripped down into the water. I closed my eyes and opened them again: it was as it had been before; grey water, grey sky, with a thin dark line where they met.

I had been there too long. That was all it was; my mind was idling, entertaining itself. It was time to go. I sat upright and attempted to fasten my seat belt, but my hands shook. I looked around for something familiar, known, and my eyes settled on the book. I picked it up and stroked it. Then I forced myself to recite:

Order – Dictyoptera.

Subgroup – Mantodea.

Families – Chaeteesidae; Metallycidae; Mantoididae; Amorphoscelidae; Eremiaphilidae; Hymenopodidae; Mantidae; Empusidae.

The two main groups in the order of Dictyoptera (Greek: diction = net; pteron = wing) *are mantids and cockroaches. In some taxonomic schemes these two suborders are listed as two separate orders.*

I repeated it over and over, forcing my mind to concentrate on the rhythm of the words, instead of tuning into the endless orchestra of chaos. Eventually, my hands stopped shaking enough for me to turn the key in the ignition.

I drove the girls to Barbara's after school, through the fields, along the path of the river. We crossed the river twice: once on the way out of the town, and once near the farmhouse up on the bank.

Barbara opened the door and Grace and Tilly carried in

143

their bags. I took my book up to my room and put it on the shelf. I checked the tanks and sprayed them, then went downstairs.

The girls were outside: Tilly on the grass by the river, Grace standing by her.

The kitchen smelled of food; Barbara had been cooking. She walked over to where I stood by the open door, and we watched Tilly running in circles until she fell over. Grace picked her up.

"You look tired, Andrew," Barbara said. "Are you sleeping?"

"A bit."

"How are the girls?"

"I don't know," I said. "They don't mention it."

Tilly ran out of the frame, out of my sight.

Barbara was silent for a while, then said, "I don't know why she let him move in. I have told her."

I nodded. "Thank you. But I don't think it'll make a difference. I just don't understand."

"No," she said. "Nor do I."

She went to the cupboard and got out some plates. "I just wish there was more I could do."

"You're doing a lot," I said. "I really appreciate it."

"I suppose," she said, "time passes and things fade. That's probably the most anyone can hope for."

So time will pass and things will fade, recede, lessen, disappear. Perhaps, I thought, the man inside the house with Rachel will become sharper and clearer as I fade away, until I cannot be seen at all.

"Andrew."

And as he gets sharper, I thought, and his outline fills the house, I will be standing on the doorstep attempting to enter the house. I will be knocking and calling, but I won't be seen or heard.

"Andrew? You look like you're a very long way away."

I looked at Barbara. "What?"

"You weren't with me."

"No."

"Are you all right?" she asked.

I attempted a smile and nodded. Then I stepped outside into the air and looked out over the rough ground and the water. The girls were there, my girls. My girls.

The mantid's eyes, as always, followed me as I walked across the room. The science was one thing: the compound eye registering movement across the ommatidia, sending messages into the brain, the eyes reaching round 180 degrees, the most effective of any insect. But in addition to the science was the uncanny effect those eyes could have on whoever was caught in their sights. The feeling of unease at being watched with such precision, the black central dot in the eye apparently following my every gesture and movement.

Ever-watchful. Ever-observant. Omniscient.

I lifted the lid and dropped in a medium-sized cricket. The mantid watched, with a quality of stillness unmatched in the natural world.

★

After eating, Barbara took a bottle of wine into the living room, and we sat on the sofa. She put on some music and I listened, carefully following each note, each rise and fall, attempting to keep my mind on the one thing, keep it still. Focused. Ever-present.

"Andrew," she said, "I'm worried about you."

I followed the swoop of the music, the subsequent dip down and then the steady rhythm that echoed my heart and my breathing, the swelling of my lungs. The pump of my blood.

"Andrew. Are you listening?"

I turned to her. "Yes," I said. "I'm worried about myself as well."

She was staring at me and it felt as though she could see too much. I thought again of the man in Rachel's house becoming clearer, as I became blurred and softened.

"Andrew. What do you mean?" she asked. "You have to explain."

"Nothing," I said. "It was a joke."

"It wasn't."

I shifted still further so I faced her completely. "It was, honestly."

"Would you say if it wasn't?" she asked. "Would you tell me if you really were concerned? I just have no idea what you're thinking."

"I'd say," I promised.

She shrugged. "That's something, I suppose." She stood up and changed the music.

In the brief silence I looked out of the window. I tried

to concentrate on the view, but as before when I'd seen the horizon move, an image appeared in my mind. The triangular head of the mantis, a cricket's leg hanging out of its mouth.

And behind it, a yellow bird.

The mantid seizes the locust, but does not see the yellow bird behind him.

I could hear the mandibles closing on the cricket's body, could hear as the mantis bit down into the exoskeleton. I shook my head quickly, wanting to rid myself of both the image and sound, but it felt as though the mantis, the cricket and the yellow bird were in there, objects rolling across the floor of my head, banging into the sides of my skull.

I picked up my wine glass and drained, then refilled it. I drank again, softening and deadening what was beginning to creep into my mind.

The curtains were drawn back and the morning light fell through them and hit my face, rousing me from a deep sleep.

I lay there for a few moments before opening my eyes. I searched for the green walls and the uneven texture on the ceiling, then gradually realized where I was. The empty bottles on the table, the half-full glasses. My mind, my memory, was vague and clouded. I felt a weight on my leg and saw Barbara lying on the sofa with me. My body was still, my mind desperately running through the blurred contents to see how we had ended up there. I remembered starting the bottle of wine, remembered talking and then needing to drink more, until I had begun to lose control. Had I cried? I had a memory of crying, but no understanding of why, nor of why I had not gone to bed.

I didn't hear the door, but I did hear Tilly calling for me, "Dad. Dad." And on the second Dad, the word falling away. And the door closing behind her as she left the room.

I stood up and staggered slightly, my balance unsteady, the alcohol still in my system. My head hurt and I was dehydrated. I smoothed my hair down before crossing the room to the door.

In the kitchen, Tilly sat at the table and Grace stood by the worksurface, her back to me.

I walked to the sink to get a glass of water. Grace turned and saw me there; she threw down the knife she held, and left the room. There were some headache tablets on the bottom shelf of the cupboard and I swallowed two; one got caught in my throat and I began to gag. I drank the remains of the glass of water, and managed to dislodge it.

I wiped my mouth and forehead and went to leave the room, but Tilly spoke. "Dad," she said, "you promised I could have pancakes. You promised."

"I know. I'll do it."

I bent to get the bowl from the cupboard and it felt as though my brain was adrift in my skull, reminding me of the previous night: the mantis, the cricket and the yellow bird, stuck in my head, rolling around. I forced myself to think through what I needed: flour, eggs, milk, butter for frying. I mixed together the flour and eggs and milk, and lumps started to form. I stopped stirring and drank more water.

The door to the kitchen opened and Grace walked in. She took something from the table and went to go again. "Grace," I said.

She glared at me, then spun on her heels and stamped out. I heard the front door slam.

"She's cross," Tilly said, "because you were in there with Barbara."

"Oh no." I shook my head. "Tilly, she doesn't understand. Stay there." I dropped the whisk into the bowl and moved quickly out of the kitchen, into the hall and out of the front door. Grace was already walking down the road. I called out and she half stopped but then continued. I called again. This time she stopped and turned back.

I ran towards her, in my socks; my brain adrift again, banging against the sides of my skull.

"Where are you going?"

"Anywhere, as long as it's not here or with Mum."

"You don't understand," I said. "Nothing happened."

She shook her head. "You're just as bad as her."

"Listen to me," I said. "You've jumped to a conclusion."

She stared at me, then shrugged. "I just want to be on my own," she said.

So I let her go.

★

In the kitchen I found Barbara cooking the pancakes. Tilly was standing by the door into the garden. Barbara turned to me. "Where have you been?"

"He ran after Grace," Tilly said. "She was cross cos you were asleep with Daddy."

Barbara tipped out the last pancake. "I see," she said. "Well, your sister has no need to be cross at all. We fell asleep, had too many glasses of wine, which was naughty. You've fallen asleep on the sofa before, haven't you?"

"When I was a child."

Barbara laughed. "Here. Take this one and go and play outside."

Tilly did as she was told and Barbara carried two cups of tea over to the table. "Sit down," she said. "I hope you don't feel as bad as I do."

"I feel dreadful," I said.

"You got quite upset last night."

I looked down at the table. "I was drunk."

"I did notice."

We sat in silence for a while, which was a relief as I'm not sure I could actually have spoken at that moment. I felt a swelling in my head as if water had been added to my brain until it reached bursting point. As though it would split open and the objects in my mind would spill out, fall on to the table. I stood up, unable to cope with the unbearable internal pressure, and walked to the doors and leaned my head against the cold glass.

"Andrew."

The glass on my forehead and the coldness of it.

"Andrew."

I could only just hear her voice; she had moved a long way away. I wanted to go home, to be back in my reading chair with the cushions stacked behind me and the books in their pile, and my insects in the outside shed.

"I can't stay here," I said.

"Of course you can."

"No," I said. "I'll find somewhere else. I won't be in your way much longer."

"Don't say that."

"I'm sorry," I said, and left the room.

The mantid's eyes swivelled round, following my movements. I lifted the lid and placed another, larger cricket in the tank. She paused, watched, then seized, the action again too fast for my eyes to register; the evidence was in her pincers, offered up to her mouth. She methodically ate its still-twitching body until even that had gone.

I took the male from his tank and placed him in with the now-full female. I closed the lid and watched them through the glass, forcing myself to concentrate, making myself repeat, repeat, repeat:

Order – Dictyoptera.

Subgroup – Mantodea.

Families – Chaeteesidae; Metallycidae; Mantoididae; Amorphoscelidae; Eremiaphilidae; Hymenopodidae; Mantidae; Empusidae.

Dictyoptera is closely related to the orders of Orthoptera, Phasmida, Isoptera and Dermaptera.

All Pterygotes. The prefix *ptera*, meaning winged. As opposed to Apterygotes, the primitive, wingless insects whom evolution passed by.

In China, the consumption of the roast egg cases, the ootheca, will cure bed-wetting.

In France, if a child is lost, the mantid will point the way home.

In Africa, the mantid will land on the dead and bring them back to life.

They pray towards Mecca.

They are the worshippers of God.

The consumers of the male after the sexual act.

Praying. Preying.

There was a knock on the door, which I ignored, then another knock and the door slowly opened. Barbara entered. I kept my eyes firmly towards the floor.

"Andrew," she said.

She waited but I said nothing, refused to look up.

"I've sent Tilly next door. She's playing with their daughter." She waited again for a response but I still said nothing. "Andrew. We just had too much to drink and fell asleep. Grace will realize. I'll talk to her."

I didn't move. Remained still. A quality of stillness unmatched in the natural world.

Barbara walked over to the tanks. "I called Rachel. I told her Grace was upset and she's going to get her. She can't have gone far. Tilly didn't want to go with them, so

I'll look after her. You can have a quiet day here." She put her hand on my shoulder. "Come on, come and have a coffee. Something to eat."

I pushed her away. "Please," I said. "I just need to be on my own."

She sighed, then quietly left the room.

In France, if a child is lost, the mantid will point the way home.

In Africa, the mantid will land on the dead and bring them back to life.

They pray towards Mecca.

They are the worshippers of God.

The consumers of the male after the sexual act.

Praying. Preying.

I sat in the car and stared at the water, watched the surface move with the tidal pull, willed it to take me and return me to the simplicity of the basic elements before me: water, earth, sky.

I listened to myself breathing, struggling to get the air in and out. I was aware of each breath from my mouth to my lungs, then from my diaphragm, up into my chest, my throat. I knew if I didn't concentrate on the process, I would never breathe again.

Here again, this place. Water, earth, sky.

I pulled the rear-view mirror round towards me. My eyes were red, bloodshot. One central black pupil letting in light to form a single image on the retina, which is converted by nerve cells into a pattern of impulses to be transmitted down the optic nerve right into the brain.

The mantid's eye, the compound eye, made up of the ommatidia, the visual receptors. Each ommatidium consists of the lens, a crystalline cone, visual cells, pigment cells. As objects move across the eyes, the ommatidia are switched on and off, giving a flicker effect. The composite of the responses of the ommatidia creates a mosaic image, and the quality of that image is dependent upon the number of ommatidia; the more images, the clearer the overall picture.

Here again, this place. Water, earth, sky.

Later, back at the house, I recall sitting in the kitchen, watching Tilly making a sheet of aluminium foil into animals, shaping it into heads and legs and tails.

I was the objective observer. A degree of separation between myself and what was occurring within the room.

The telephone rang and the sound of it was disjointed, jarring. I heard Barbara speaking, heard her words as though they were a piece of music to accompany the ringing that I could still hear though another part of me realized it had in fact stopped.

"Andrew?"

I looked up at her standing above me, her apron tied around her waist, her face smiling.

"Grace is fine. Back at home. Tilly's staying here on her own, aren't you?"

"Yes," Tilly said. She held up one of the silver animals and Barbara took it, examined it.

"It's lovely. Now, come on, let's get you up to bed."

"I'm taking all of these." Tilly carefully collected up her foil animals to take with her.

"Give Daddy a kiss."

Tilly kissed me on the cheek, then said, "Why aren't you putting me to bed?"

"Daddy has a headache," Barbara said before I could speak. "And I wanted to make sure your animals are all right up there."

Tilly nodded and followed Barbara from the room.

It was silent when they had gone, and I noticed my legs and hands were shaking. I listened to the sounds in my head, the ringing and the rhythm of words.

When Barbara came back down, she finished cooking and asked me to sit at the table.

"How are you?" she asked as she served the food.

"I'm fine."

"Andrew, I don't believe you are."

"No, I am." I drank from the glass of water she'd placed before me. "Believe me."

"Did you mean it, that you're not staying?"

I nodded. "I think it's best if I find my own place."

"I don't know why. You're much better here. I can keep an eye on you."

"I'm just a nuisance. I can't do anything at the moment. Can't do anything right for them. You don't need me here, being like this."

"You're fine here."

She smiled, but I could tell she didn't mean it, that she'd be relieved if I did move out.

"Andrew?" she said. "Did you hear me?"

I shook my head.

"I didn't think so. I said that when I've spoken to Grace and she understands, it'll be fine."

I pushed my plate away, barely touched, and stood up.

"Where are you going?"

"I'm sorry," I said. "I'm just not hungry."

"You have to eat. Look how thin you are."

"I'll eat tomorrow. I want to go to bed and read."

"All right. Look, it will all be fine, Andrew. It will."

"Will it?" I asked. "It's all so much more difficult and complicated than you think."

She said nothing, just looked at me.

"Much more. Much, much more."

"Andrew, you're shouting."

"I'm not."

"You are. Please. Calm down."

"I am calm." I stood there a for a second, forcing myself to slow my breathing, then I spoke. "I'm sorry," I said.

"It's okay."

"I'll see you in the morning."

Tilly was asleep, her thumb wedged firmly in her mouth. The foil animals were in ordered lines on the floor, and a new doll lay at the bottom of the bed. I picked it up and turned it over in my hands, then saw her hair was missing, leaving empty holes in the pink plastic scalp. Tilly had wrapped the strands of hair into a circle, a synthetic nest that she'd put beside her on the pillow; inside it a foil animal.

I went down the wooden stairs and into my room where I sat on the carpet and listened to my breathing. I drew my legs to my chest and rested my head on my knees, pressing my eyes hard against them to block out any images, but they still came, looming large in my mind.

Praying towards Mecca.

Worshipping God.

Consuming males after the sexual act.

Praying. Preying.

I jumped up, went to the tank and lifted the lid. The female held her front raptorial legs together in prayer. Her eyes followed my movements as I searched for the male under the leaves and branches.

Nothing.

I replaced the lid.

I had never previously forgotten to remove the male immediately after mating.

The following morning I took Tilly home. She had her foil animals on her lap and walked one of them across the dashboard.

I drove carefully, keeping to the left of the road, finding

it helpful to repeat the rule: drive on the left and listen for passing cars. Listen for passing cars and listen to each and every breath. Inhale, exhale.

"Dad," Tilly said, trotting the animal towards me, "why are you driving so fast?"

"I'm not."

The foil animal slid from her grasp as I braked to avoid a car coming towards us, the horn blowing. We slowed to a halt and sat in silence for a while. Tilly looked at me. "Are you okay?"

"I'm fine," I snapped.

"Then why aren't we moving?"

I pulled out into the road again and continued. "We are now."

Tilly retrieved her animal from the floor and held it tightly in her lap with the others.

I stopped the car outside my old home and sat listening to the ticking of the cooling engine and my own breathing.

I looked down and saw a small clump of hairs in Tilly's hands. She fiddled with them, threading them through her fingers.

I picked up her bag and we started towards the house.

It was Rachel who opened the door. She stared at me. Tilly ran under her arm and disappeared; I handed Rachel her bag.

"What is it?" she asked. "What's the matter?"

"Nothing."

"Then take your hand off the bell," she said.

I laughed and moved my hand and the noise stopped.

"What is it?" she asked. "What do you want?"

"Can I come in?"

"No."

I saw a movement in the hall behind her and then the man came into view.

"Let me in. Please."

"No, Andrew. No."

She closed the door and I stood there, my breathing beginning to catch in my throat, the lack of air, and I started banging on the wood of the door. Banging and banging, my breathing getting lost, and my heart racing and jumping.

Tilly

When you pull out a hair it has a lump on one end where it was stuck in a hole in your head. The other end is straight across if it has been cut but sometimes there are hairs which have not been cut and they are new ones and they have a point. The cut ones feel nice when you poke them on your finger.

And if you have your thumb in your mouth and suck hard and have some of the straight cut ones and poke them on your nose that feels even nicer.

Noses are in the middle of faces. Faces are important. When I am standing, I can't see faces. Children can see legs and they can see the floor easily.

My dad was outside the house and my mum was inside. When my mum answered the door I couldn't see their faces but I knew they wouldn't be smiling. I ran under her arm and went into the house and up the stairs to find Grace but she was coming down to see what all the noise was.

Insects don't have hair.

They have crispy skin and lots of legs. They have separate bits, called segments.

Oranges have segments but I don't like oranges much.

Rachel

We were in the kitchen together, washing up, when the doorbell began ringing, short bursts at first, then insistent.

Dave turned to me and asked who it was.

'How do I know? I haven't answered the door yet,' I said as I walked down the hall, the bell still ringing. I saw his shape through the frosted glass and called out, 'All right. All right,' then opened the door. He was standing there, his breathing loud and rapid, Tilly beside him. She ran under my arm into the house, and Andrew held out her bag, which I took.

'What is it?' I asked. 'What's the matter?'

'Nothing,' he said. His breathing was so laboured.

'Then take your hand off the bell,' I said.

He laughed, and it was like his breathing, out of control. He moved his hand and the ringing finally stopped.

'What is it?' I asked. 'What do you want?'

For the first time he met my eyes. 'Can I come in?'

His eyes were bloodshot and dark underneath. I was about to step back and let him in when I heard Dave behind me.

'No,' I said, and started to close the door.

'Let me in. Please.'

'No, Andrew. No.'

He put his hand out but I ignored it. My heart was beating too fast now, and I rested my head on the closed door.

Then it began, him banging on the door, over and over.

Grace leaned over the banisters. 'What is it?'

'It's your dad,' I said. 'I'll have to let him in, see if he's all right.'

'What's his problem?' Dave said. 'I don't want him here.'

'It's bloody nothing to do with you,' Grace shouted.

'Don't you speak to me like that,' Dave was saying as I pushed him down the hall towards the kitchen. 'Please,' I said. 'Something's not right.'

'He's putting it on,' he said. 'Trying for the sympathy vote.'

'Five minutes,' I said. 'Then he'll have to go.'

Dave sighed.

'Please,' I said. 'Five minutes. I'll tell you when he's gone.'

He shrugged. 'Five minutes. I'll be in the garden.'

I opened the door. 'Rachel,' Andrew said, 'I can't breathe.'

'You'd better come in.'

I led him into the kitchen and pulled out a chair.

'Sit there,' I said. 'Just try and breathe deeply. That's it.' He struggled to get up but I told him to sit still.

For a few minutes there was just the sound of his desperate breathing. When it had finally steadied, I asked, 'What's going on?'

He shook his head.

'Something is,' I said. 'This isn't normal.'

He sat there, said nothing.

'Andrew. Why did Barbara ask me to pick up Grace yesterday?'

He looked down at the floor.

'Something must have happened.'

He glanced at me. 'Nothing happened.' His eyes were wet, strangely blank. I filled a glass of water, gave it to him.

'Look,' I said, 'I don't think the girls should be staying with you.'

He looked up instantly. 'No.'

'Not if you're like this, in this state.'

'I'm not in a state.'

I looked at him sitting there, thin where he'd lost too much weight, his skin pale. 'Andrew.'

'I'm fine.' He stood up, but held tightly on to the back of the chair for support.

'You're not fine,' I said. 'I'm not sure you're fit to have them.'

'Don't say that.' Suddenly he was right in front of me, shouting. A speck of saliva landed on my cheek and I wiped it off. 'Don't say that.'

'Don't shout at me.' I spoke slowly and clearly. 'If you're going to be like this, I'll call the police.'

'No. Please, no.'

'Or I'll have to contact the solicitor and say you aren't fit to have them.'

He stopped. Was silent for a moment. Still.

Grace came in. She must have been in the hall, heard every word.

'Listen to you both,' she said. 'You make me sick.' She left and we heard the front door slam behind her.

I turned to Andrew. 'Now see what you've done.'

He shook his head. 'I didn't do it. You did.'

'Because I couldn't live with you any more?'

He nodded. 'Yes. Yes.'

In the garden, I saw Dave getting up out of his chair. I turned back.

'I want you to go,' I said.

He shook his head again and his hair flopped on to his face. 'No.'

'I said I want you to go.'

'And I said no.'

'This is not your house.'

He stared at me. 'It was my house. I found it. I painted it. I did everything in this house.'

'It's just a house,' I said.

'Is it? Just a house? Do you know what I've lost?' He took a step closer to me. Too close.

'Look,' I said quietly, and I reached out to touch him. 'I understand.'

He leaped back. 'Don't touch me. Don't fucking touch me.'

I raised my hands. I had never heard him speak like that. Never. 'I only wanted to say I understand how you feel.'

'No,' he said. 'You don't know how I feel. No one does.'

Dave appeared, his sunglasses pushed up on top of his head. 'What's going on?' he asked.

'Nothing,' I said.

Dave put his hand on Andrew's shoulder. 'You need some help finding the door?'

'Don't, Dave,' I said.

'Well, he looks like he might not know the way out.'

'Please don't, Dave.'

Andrew looked at me. His red, glassy eyes. Pleading. 'Don't make me go,' he said.

'Come on.' I gestured towards the door. To Dave, I added, 'Leave it. He's just going.'

He gave a small shrug, realizing by my tone how serious I was. 'He's got to be gone in two minutes,' Dave said, then headed back outside.

Andrew waited until we were alone again. 'What happened? Have you forgotten everything?'

I said nothing.

'Have you forgotten,' he asked, 'how happy we were once? Because we were. I know we were.'

'I really don't want this conversation,' I said. 'You have to go.'

'Rachel.'

'No. I have nothing more to say.'

'Why is he here?' he asked. 'Why's that man here?'

'Because I want him here.'

'Do you?' He stared at me intently. 'Do you really?'

I looked away. 'You get on with your own life,' I said. 'I'll get on with mine.'

'And the girls? What do they think about him being here?'

I walked past him into the hall. Opened the front door. A passing car drowned out his next words.

'Please go,' I said.

'Rachel. There were times when we were happy.'

'No,' I said. The word came out quickly. Sharply. 'Andrew, we've discussed all this. It's all too late. We need to move on. Let go.'

'But I can't.'

He tried to take my hand, but I stepped back, away from him.

'I have to move on in my life,' I said. 'Why can't you understand that?'

'Who is he? How well do you know him?'

It was then I began to lose my composure. 'That's enough,' I snapped. 'You have to go.'

'No.'

'You have to,' I said, and put my hand on his arm and pushed. I didn't mean to push hard, but he staggered and grabbed hold of the rail to stop himself falling right down.

'Rachel,' he said.

I closed the door. He wouldn't have stopped otherwise. I slid the bolt and stood there while he stood on the other side, banging the door over and over, his fist against the wood. But this time I wasn't going to open it.

I ran upstairs and sat on the chair on the landing. Away from the door and away from Andrew. I tucked my hands between my legs to stop them shaking.

How did all this happen?

The banging on the door ended, and Dave called up the stairs. 'Rach. You okay?'

'I'm fine,' I said. 'I'll be down in a minute.'

I stood up and smoothed my skirt, brushed myself down. Ran my fingers through my hair. I walked along the landing and was about to turn down the stairs when I saw Tilly's bedroom door was open. She lay on her floor, her fingers curled into her hair. She was lifting her head and bringing it down, hard, on the carpet.

'What are you doing?' I said. 'Don't do that.'

I ran into the room and knelt beside her, took her face in my hands.

She stared at me. 'I hate you,' she said. 'I want Dad.'

Then I saw a patch at the front of her head where her hair was missing and the skin was red and raw.

'What've you done, Til?'

She escaped from under my hands and got away, ran out of the room. I could hear her footsteps on the stairs. I had two daughters, and they were both running away from me.

I knelt there for a while, then stood up. On her bed

there was a row of silver foil shapes and her book, open in the middle. I looked at the image of the girl in the red dress seen through the glass of the tank, and the praying mantis smiling at her. Smiling at the girl? I thought. Smiling? The insect would eat her, piece by piece. Grip her by the neck and begin to eat, until her body stopped twitching.

I left the room and turned to go down the stairs, thinking I would find Tilly and talk to her, force her to talk to me. As I passed Grace's room, I stopped. Her door was closed and I turned the handle and pushed it open.

On the wall, the black letters she'd painted there, the initial letter H in red and gold and green.

He shall be like a tree planted by the rivers of water.

I stepped closer and reached out, touched the letter with the tip of my finger, and the black line smudged and the green powder fell in a shower of dust.

Her voice startled me. 'What are you doing in here?'

I turned and saw her in the doorway, watching me.

'Nothing,' I said. I gestured at the writing. 'Why are you doing this?'

She ignored me and walked over to the cage and took out the bird.

'What's going on?' I asked. 'Grace. Please.'

She sat down on the floor, the bird on her lap. Feathered now, it made a low, rhythmical sound and she rubbed its head. 'All right,' she said in a quiet, calming voice. 'It's coming.' She picked up the bread she'd soaked and the bird opened its beak and swallowed.

'I thought you weren't going to handle it,' I said.

I waited but she didn't answer, just took another piece of bread and fed it to the bird.

'From now on,' I said, 'you have to stay here and go to school every day. No more running away. No more going to your father's. And no more going down to that David's house to do God knows what.'

She placed the bird on the floor and it stretched its wings. 'What is it you think I'm doing down there?' she asked. 'Go on. Say it.'

'I won't have that argument again. It's just you're still young,' I said. 'You need to let me know where you're going.'

'Why?'

'Because I'm responsible for your well-being.'

She laughed, a high, brittle laugh I had never heard before. 'Then you're not doing a very good job, are you?'

I waited for a second, took a deep breath. 'It's easy from where you are to see it. Easy to see what everyone else should do.'

Grace stood up and slipped the bird back into its cage. She turned to me. 'You know what?' she said. 'I've had enough of being understanding and seeing it from everyone else's point of view. I just want to see it from mine. I'd like to be on my own now. Can you go? Please.'

'No,' I said.

'What exactly is it you think I'm doing down there?'

'I'm not stupid,' I said.

'You know something? We're not all like you and Dad.'

'What,' I asked, 'is that supposed to mean?'

'I've heard you with him,' she said. 'And now I'm going to have to hear Dad with Barbara.'

I stared at her. 'What?'

'You heard.'

'Barbara wouldn't do that. Nor Andrew.'

She laughed at me, that high laugh again. 'No? Well, if that makes you feel better, you just keep telling yourself that.' She gestured at the door. 'Ask him, why don't you? Ask why Tilly found them both on the sofa in the morning, lying there together.'

I shook my head. Dave called my name from downstairs.

'I think someone wants you,' Grace said.

In bed that night I turned out my light and lay still, unable to sleep. Everything ran around and around my mind.

Around my mind. Around and around.

Dave turned over in the bed and rested his hand on my belly. 'Rach,' he said quietly. 'I'm thinking of getting another tattoo.'

'Where?'

'Here. On the inside of my arm. What do you think?'

'I don't know,' I said.

'Rach.' He paused for a second, then, 'I want your name on there.'

My body stopped working for a second.

'What do you think?'

'No,' I said. But I said it so softly, it was almost like breathing, the response came from somewhere so deep, and he didn't hear me.

I thought of my name on his skin, the letters seeping down under his skin, into his body.

Writing on his skin.

'Rach,' he said. He started moving his hand in circles on my belly. Round and round, then he cupped my breast. I pushed his hand away.

He spoke quietly again, the words hot, right into my ear. 'What? What is it?'

'Nothing,' I said. 'I'm just tired.'

He ran his hand down between my legs. I pushed it away again. He turned on his bedside light and sat up. 'What is it?'

'I said, nothing.'

'It's him. It's since he came here.'

'I don't know who you're talking about,' I said.

'Him. Andrew.' He pulled my shoulder to turn me towards him. 'You know what? You're too bloody good to him. You shouldn't have let him in. Unless you still have feelings for him.'

I shook my head. 'You don't understand,' I said.

'Oh no. That's just it. I do understand. I understand exactly. You should be looking after your interests. Yours and mine.'

I continued to shake my head. 'No.'

'Yes.'

'And my girls?' I asked. 'What about their interests?'

He spoke quickly. 'Fuck your girls.'

I stared at him, then shook my head again, horrified. 'You can't say that.'

He was silent for a second, then put his hand on my face, stroked me. 'I didn't mean that. You know I didn't. Rach. I really didn't mean it.'

'Didn't you?' I said. I brushed his hand away and got out of the bed.

In the garden, I could smell the dry summer grass and the white jasmine round the door. Could see the white of the flowers, even in the dark. I sat on the wooden chair and watched the clouds drift across the moon.

Then, later, I went to the bottom of the garden and let myself through the gate. I walked to the end of the road and turned down the hill, towards the river. I stood on the bank and listened to the dark water.

The thoughts in my head moved too quickly for me to grasp and I let them run freely through my mind. The trees were dark silhouettes in the night sky, and the air smelled sweet. I took my shoes and socks off and let the air creep between my toes. Took my skirt off and let the air wrap round my legs. Took my shirt off and let the air touch me.

I meant only to slip my toe in, to feel the temperature of the water, but as the cold hit my skin, I lay down and wriggled forward till both of my legs were in the water. I inched forward, entering further, the feel of the cold like a vice, clamping my waist and sucking at my body, enveloping me with the mud and water and earth. My feet touched the bottom and the smooth silt filled the spaces between my toes.

I pushed myself away from the bank, my eyes closed. My breathing stopped. I pushed further and put my head under the water and floated. The cold contracted my scalp and I felt my body tighten. Weed wrapped itself round my legs, and the water filled me.

I thought of Andrew in my kitchen, his breathing hard and fast, his lack of control. Tilly with her red, sore skin. The writing on the walls, the green powder raining down. Dave, wanting my name on his skin, the ink sinking deep into the layers. And I thought of what Grace had told me. Barbara, curling up to Andrew, filling the space I had left by his side.

How had it all come to this?

We were lost. All of us lost.

I lay on the bank and the water dripped from my body on to the grass. The smell of the earth and water, a metallic note, stayed on me, and I licked my arm and tasted it. Earth and water. Water and earth.

I was cold now, shivering, covered in goose bumps. I pulled my clothes on as quickly as I could, the fabric snagging against my chilled skin. I needed to get home, wanted to see Tilly, touch her hot, sleeping body. Check on Grace.

And then Andrew's words came back to me: There were times when we were happy.

I had shaken my head, denying there were any. But

there were times, I knew that. One of them here, a hot sunny day, lying on the blanket, before we had children, when our bodies had curved towards each other and we swam in this very river, and touched each other under water, our legs round each other's waists.

They shall fear thee as long as the sun and moon endure,
throughout all generations.

He shall come down like rain upon the mown grass:
as showers that water the earth.

In his days shall the righteous flourish; and abundance
of peace so long as the moon endureth.

He shall have dominion also from sea to sea, and from
the river unto the ends of the earth.

Grace

The table was laid. A white tablecloth and a glass bowl of raspberries from the garden. Fresh bread and cheese and deep yellow butter. His mother poured tea into thin cups, spooned in white sugar. We ate in silence.

My heart beat slowly and calmly, and my bird slept in her box.

—We were waiting for you, she said when we had finished. —I told you that you would come back.

She took me through to the hall. Pots of paint lay on the floor. Newspaper with a pile of brushes and pencils.

I held the book in my left hand and turned the pages, looked through until I found the words I wanted. I chose a pencil and slowly wrote, dragging the lead across the raw plaster:

As the hart panteth after the water brooks, so panteth my soul after thee, O God.

I took the paints and filled in the initial letter A, until the pencil marks had gone and the colour said what I wanted it to.

Then I picked up the pencil again and drew underneath the words. A hart, its body large and clumsy, its four legs racing across the land towards the water. Spots on its side, and antlers. I took the red powder paint and rubbed it on, pressed colour into the plaster. Used the gold to fill in the shape of the antlers.

When we had finished David walked me to the end of the garden and we sat under the willow. The branches dipped down into the water and were dragged along by the current. I looked at my hand. The red pigment and gold leaf had sunk into my skin. I looked at David. In the sun, his hair glinted red and gold, the same colour as my hand. It was so different here. The peace and certainty. Everything else seemed far away, as though this was all there was.

I took the bird from the box. She was wary of the grass at first, then slowly began to experiment, lifting her feet and circling.

We both watched her for a while, then David spoke. — You should be at school. Your family must be worried about you.

I said nothing. I watched the bird making larger circles, stopping, tipping her head to one side.

—Grace, he said, —tell me what's happening.

I didn't answer straight away. I wanted to keep all that deep below, in a separate place from him, this river, and the writing on the walls. But he asked again, and so I told him what he needed to know, about the man in Mum's bed, about Dad and Barbara, that we were being passed from house to house, and how I couldn't stand any of it.

A pair of damselflies hovered above the water, their wings metallic blue. A clump of weed floated downstream.

He spoke, eventually, asked me how my dad was.

I smoothed the bird's feathers and scratched her head. —Not good, I said. —I worry about him. He keeps going to the river, right to the end where it flows out to sea. He just sits and stares at the water.

—He'll be all right. Someone is keeping an eye on him.

—You believe that? I asked. —You really believe it?

—Of course I do.

—I wish I did, I said.

—You could if you wanted to.

But could I? I wasn't sure, however much I would like to, however much the certainties appealed to me. I thought of the words on the walls, the sure way they were written, the absolute, unquestionable state of them. And there in the book too, the words so clear, so confident. Black and white. And yet—.

—You could, he said again. —If you wanted to.

I shook my head. —I don't believe anyone's looking after us. How could all this have happened to me? And my sister?

—Do you think all this is random? You think that everything that happens is unconnected?

I nodded.

—Grace, he said. —Why were you there when I fell?

I smiled. —I just was.

—Don't you see how that sounds? Things don't happen in an unconnected way like that. It's all part of a pattern. It's just a matter of whether you can see it or not.

—If that's the case, I asked, —what about what you did to yourself the day I found you? If you believe there's a pattern, and things are how they're meant to be, why did you do that?

He stopped smiling immediately and looked away, at the water, said nothing for a bit, then, —I used to help your dad in his classroom.

—He told me. He remembered you.

—Did he? I used to go there to escape. They didn't make it easy for me to go to school.

—Why?

—I think they saw something in me I hadn't recognized myself. Not then, anyway.

—What?

He didn't answer, but picked up the bird. He scratched her head as I had done, and extended her wings to examine her new, long feathers. He placed her back on the grass and she stretched, and straightened her wings again, running her beak along them to correct the feathers.

—He was good to me, he said. —He taught me a lot. He gave me one of his old tanks and I kept crickets, just to watch them. I don't know if he realized how important he was to me.

—What happened to your dad? I asked.

—I never knew him. He died before I was born.

—I'm sorry.

—It's okay. It's just the way it was meant to be. These things are tests, to see if you're strong enough.

—You really believe that? I asked.

—Yes. You see, the day you found me, I wasn't strong enough. I felt I was failing Him.

—But why that day? What had happened?

He shook his head and shifted on to his stomach. I looked at his hand, which was brown from the sun and covered in pale hairs. I moved my hand towards his, but he pulled away quickly. Too quickly.

—Don't touch me, he said. —Don't touch me.

After a few moments I put the bird back in her box and carefully closed the flaps, tucking them in one under the other.

—I'm sorry, he said.

—It's okay, I said, kneeling up to watch the river. When I thought it was safe, I glanced at him lying there, his face turned away from me. I thought about what he'd said. Him finding sanctuary in Dad's classroom at school. And him not wanting to be touched. Not by me, anyway. Not by a girl.

—David, I said. —Did my dad know?

He looked at me and must have guessed what I had worked out. He shrugged.

—Did you talk to him?

He shook his head. —I've never told anyone.

I was silent for a while, considering. Then I said, — David, if you believe there's a pattern, this must be part of it. You have to be who you are.

He shook his head again. —How can I be? The book says I'm wrong. They said at school I was wrong. It was only with your dad I got any peace.

—Why with him?

—Because he accepted I was who I was.

I nodded. We sat there for a long time without saying anything else. Then he stood up.

—Would you do it again? I asked. —Would you be that desperate again?

He thought about it. Then, —I don't think so. I like to think you were there for a reason. Perhaps I owe you something now.

He walked to the water's edge. Held on to the branch of the willow. I thought of the hart I'd drawn on the wall, its four legs racing across the land towards the water. And the words he had written beneath. *We hanged our harps upon the willows.*

David turned to me. —Come on, he said. —I'm going to call your dad and let him know where you are.

He held his hand out and I took it and he pulled me up.

Dad drove to his usual spot: down the lane, to the end of the road and the end of the stretch of land, to the river's mouth. He parked the car and we got out. I followed him through a gap in the fence and we walked across the scrubby grass, and stopped close to the edge of the water, which stretched brown-grey in front of us.

We walked along for a bit, then beside the sea, among

the stones and washed-up pieces of wood. I kicked a rusted cigarette lighter and turned over an old sandal with my foot; Dad's hair blew in the wind and his face looked thin, his eyes watery as though he had been crying.

—Are you all right? I asked.

He nodded and wiped his eyes. —It's the wind and the fresh air.

I watched a gull land, its feet sinking down into the silt.

—What happened with Barbara, he said, —it was innocent. You have to know that. You really do.

His voice was high, desperate.

—I don't know, I said.

—If I've ever said anything truthful to you, this is it.

The gull pecked at something it had found in the mud. It cried out and another gull came from the sky to join it.

—Dad. I can't stand him there. I can't stand any of this.

—No, he said. —I know.

—You have to talk to her, I said.

—I can't, he said, his voice quiet.

He stopped walking.

—Look, Grace, he said. —There's something I want to say. I want to say sorry.

A cormorant stood on top of a nearby post, its feathers stretched out to dry in the weak sunlight. A long, low container ship moved slowly through the water.

—I'm sorry for what's happened. For all of it.

I stared at the ship, at the pale blue containers piled on the deck, patches of red rust.

—And I'm sorry for being me. The two of you deserve better.

—Don't say that, I said. The gull lifted off and flew past the cormorant, towards the open sea. —You don't know how good you've been. Not just to us either. Sometimes you don't know how good you've been to people.

—No. I have to say it. I've let you down.

He walked away, still skirting the edge of the water. I followed, and we walked without speaking until we came to some mounds of dry grass, where we sat and stared into the distance. I ran my hand through the sandy earth, then dug deeper till I found a springtail.

—Member of the Apterygota subclass, Dad said when I showed him. —Virtually no metamorphosis during their life-cycle.

—Dad, I said.

—Apterygota as opposed to the Pterygote. No compound eye, unlike the mantid.

—Dad.

I looked at him. There were dark shadows beneath his eyes, and I could see he really had lost weight.

—Dad, I said. —Have you been sleeping?

He picked up a stone and weighed it in his hand. I waited.

I tried again. —Have you been sleeping?

—No. I've had some problems.

—Have you seen the doctor?

—There's no need for that, he said. —Really.

—Dad, I said.

He threw the stone and it sank into the mud. —You shouldn't be worrying about me. I'm fine.

I pushed my sandals off and pulled my legs up to my chin, rested my face on my knees. I could feel the sun on my skin and I smelled myself, earth and silt and sun, and something that smelled as though it had come from somewhere deeper, from beneath the surface of the earth.

Dad took his shoes off too and stood up. He left his shoes beside me, the socks tucked inside, and walked a little distance away. As I watched, he bent down repeatedly, then examined whatever it was he had found. He looked like a bird, his body thin and tall and his actions repeated over and over as he stepped across the silt.

Andrew

The edge of the sea, the boundary between land and water. The littoral.

I had to keep breathing and keep looking. I picked up a stone and then another. These objects from the edge. And the objects inside my head, rolling as I moved. Banging into the sides. Threatening to spill out. The skin and my scalp, threatening to split open.

The female takes the male into her pincers. She bites off his head and begins to consume and as she does so the sperm sac continues to pump semen into her body.

I looked up and saw Grace on the grass. Watching me. Smile, just look at her and smile. Be sure to smile. Don't let anyone know the objects in your head are rolling free, adrift. Don't let anyone see the inside. Create an exoskeleton, a hard carapace round this endoskeleton, the soft skin which splits and hurts. Don't let anyone know how you feel, don't let her stop you having them, or you will be thrown into the darkness, the chasm of the long daytime hours.

Smile and repeat, repeat, repeat:

Order – Dictyoptera.

Subgroup – Mantodea.

Families – Chaeteesidae; Metallycidae; Mantoididae; Amorphoscelidae; Eremiaphilidae; Hymenopodidae; Mantidae; Empusidae.

Praying. Preying.

Grace

We drove back to Barbara's house and Dad let me in before going to collect Tilly from school, as we were both staying with him for the weekend. The door closed behind him and there was silence.

I went into the kitchen and opened the fridge, but there was nothing I wanted. I walked to the big doors and looked out over the garden. There was nothing to do. I had none of my things here, didn't even want to be here. I went upstairs to the attic room. The two beds had been made and a nightdress was lying on Tilly's pillow, still with a price tag on it. So we had new things now, for this house. Two sets of things in two houses.

I wandered around aimlessly for a bit, then went to check the insects in Dad's room. In the first tank, the mantid was still, its front legs held together as though saying a prayer. I stepped to the right and saw its huge eyes move. I stepped to the left and they moved again.

—Grace.

I turned quickly and saw Barbara in the doorway.

—Sorry, I didn't mean to make you jump.

I shrugged. —I was just looking at them.

—Or they were looking at you. It's uncanny how they follow you round.

She came further into the room.

—Grace, she said. —I want to talk to you.

—I don't want to talk to you.

—Maybe, but I have something to say to you. I want to apologize. This stupid thing that happened.

—I've already talked to him about it, I said.

—He felt terrible. I'm glad you understand. It's not easy for you and Tilly.

I shrugged.

—Look, I know you don't want to talk about it. And I know it's not ideal, none of this is. I'm just really sorry. You know I love your mum. And you two. I've known you for so long.

I nodded. I wanted to ask her to stop, but I knew if I spoke she would hear the tremble in my voice.

—I won't go on, she said. —I know you hate it.

I gave another small nod, and looked in the tank again. The mantis rotated its head and fixed the black dots of its eyes on me.

—Grace. I'm going to get something to eat. Are you hungry?

—No.

—All right. I'm on nights again, so I have to eat now. I'll be in the kitchen.

She went to leave the room and I called her name. She stopped and turned back.

—Dad isn't well, I said. —He's not himself.

—I've seen it before, she said. —With other friends who've split. You get this terrible period, then it all settles down.

—Does it? I asked.

—Yes. He'll be fine. We'll all have to keep an eye on him. Come and find me when you're ready.

When the door closed behind her, I went to the window and leaned my forehead against the glass and watched the water.

In my thoughts there were new words being stamped inside me. New connections between words. New shapes being drawn each day. Patterns in my mind. My head was filling with new things: sounds, colours, lines. An outline of a head, the curve of a neck, the muscles under the skin. Horns, antlers, teeth. All made of cells, firing in odd directions, acting according to a deeply buried instruction.

All of it being written and drawn and formed, new ideas etched deep within me. Blueprints. Plans.

On the walls, the pigment driven down into the plaster. Earth on earth. The sound of the water rushing by at the end of the garden.

And the look in my father's eyes, the dark beneath.

And the man in my mother's bed, his tattoo and the smell of him, impregnating our lives.

★

That night I put Tilly to bed. I sat with her against the pillow and held the book so we could both see the drawings.

I read from the first page, read up to the point where the girl in the red dress takes Manty home with her. Tilly yawned and I told her to sleep. As I closed the book, I caught sight of the image on the cover, the face of the mantis, with black dots in her huge eyes. Her triangular head. I'd seen it so many times before, but now I looked really closely and saw where the picture was made up of tiny dots which, when seen together, looked like solid shapes and colours.

—Grace.

—Shhhh, I said. —Go to sleep.

—When will it all be normal again?

—I don't know, I said. I picked up one of her foil animals. —Here, this one's sad, you'll have to look after him. I passed her the crumpled piece of foil.

—Can't you see it's a girl? Tilly said. —I'll have to look after *her*.

I smiled. —Go to sleep.

That night, in bed, the moonlight came through the skylights. Tilly's mouth was open and her breathing heavy.

I could smell the new carpet and the new cotton of the bedclothes. I didn't want any of this. I wanted something else and I could feel it tight inside me, this longing I couldn't quite identify.

I thought about going downstairs, out into the night air, but I couldn't move, couldn't leave the warmth of the bed.

I lay there for hours and thought back over everything that had happened. I thought about that first morning when I found Dave in bed with my mum, his tattoos showing. I thought about how I'd walked away from school and across the fields. Run away from the scene where I had found Dave, only to find David under the tree. David with his room with the tank and the single bed. David battling with his world which would not allow him to be who he was.

The painted house by the river and the words traced on the plaster, the shape of the O, the perfect circle, and the feeling I had inside when I thought of it. The colours printed deep in my mind, the words tucked under my skin as I lay beneath my white sheets. Tilly's sweet breath in the room.

As the hart panteth after the water brooks, so panteth my soul after thee, O God.

The house with its red bricks, and the river at the end of the garden. The tree and the leaves dipping down into the water. The words on the walls and the certainty of them. The link between life and death, the joining of bodies and the other, liquid things that exist inside a body, moving and shifting and trying to find words. It felt as though everything was connecting up, but I didn't know how.

★

I watched the moonlight inch across the floor. Tilly's breathing got lighter and she turned over, put her thumb in her mouth.

Then, when my own breathing finally began to change as I moved towards sleep, I heard feet on the stairs, and the front door opening and closing. There was the noise of the car door outside and I wondered what was happening, but I was now beginning to slip further into sleep. I ignored it and let myself enter the black layers, unaware that it was one of those times when, had I acted, done something, I could have changed what happened next.

O my God, I cry in the daytime, but thou hearest not.

*I am poured out like water, and all my bones are out of joint;
my heart is like wax; it is melted in the midst of my bowels.*

Mantids and Other Dictyoptera

REPRODUCTION

Reproduction begins with courtship rituals. The male performs an 'abdominal wave', bending and waving his abdomen and legs. The approach is normally tentative as, when he begins his courtship, the male does not know whether it will end in death or consummation.

The male can take up to two hours to approach the female, and he employs either one of two tactics: he can either surprise her by suddenly leaping on to her, or he can stalk her, using stealth to get close enough to jump on her back.

Whether or not cannibalism takes place depends on whether or not the female is hungry. If her appetite is satiated, it may not take place. However, if she is very hungry, cannibalism does normally occur. The female can consume the male before, during or after mating. The benefits of cannibalism during reproduction are numerous and include: the destruction of competition for other females; the rejection of a suitor; nutritional supplies for the young.

Once the sperm has been transferred from the male, the female can use some sperm for immediate fertilization, but can also retain some, in which case, it will remain viable for several months. During those months, she can consume the sperm if she needs extra nutrients or, if she wishes, she can reject it.

During cannibalization, the central nervous system allows the male to continue mating, and he will continue to pump sperm into the female. There is some recent evidence, in fact, that the partly decapitated/cannibalized male is more vigorous and effective in thrusting, and therefore is more successful at fertilization (Martin, 1983).

The Unhappy Insect

The girl in the red dress put Manty into a cardboard box, but this time there was scrunched-up tissue in there too, so that when the box was moved, she wouldn't bang against the sides.

Manty could hear an engine, and she could hear voices. Human voices.

After a long time everything stopped.

When the box was opened, the light streamed in. The box was tipped up and she slid into her new home.

It was lovely.

A nice big tank with clean earth and green leaves.

The small hand appeared and dropped in a live cricket and Manty watched it carefully before jumping on it. She held it in her praying hands, and ate it bit by bit till it was all gone.

From that day on Manty was very happy. Every morning the girl in the red dress came and lifted the lid of the tank and smiled at Manty and said 'Good morning'. She sprayed water in the tank and then every single day she put in a live cricket or moth or some flies and Manty ate everything in that tank that moved.

Andrew

I took the potatoes in my hand and ran the peeler over their bodies, slicing off the skin, checking each one for impurities. An eye. A bruise. An imperfection, only visible when stripped bare. When I finished I put them into the cold water. They were naked, white, exposed. Each one sore and damaged.

My feet were planted squarely on the floor, taking my weight evenly. Stand erect, shoulders back to open the chest cavity, and breathe. In, out. In, out. It is the breathing that is important. The correct use of the diaphragm and the musculature of the body and lungs was what was required of me. Control must be retained over the function of the inner organs of the body. I knew what I was doing finally. I had a direction, an end goal.

I took the next potato and removed the outer layer. This one had a deep grey bruise. I took more and more off but the bruise spread. I kept peeling until nothing remained. I let go, and the scrapings tumbled into the sink. The next one had a deep eye, small sprouts growing from it. My mind leaped to make the connection between the eye of the potato and my own eyes, and for a second I had an image of the convex retina over my pupil bursting open as new shoots forced their way out, slowly unfurling, the green leaves and stems trailing down my face. I shook my head to rid myself of the thought.

At that moment, Grace tapped me on the shoulder. I took a breath, then turned.

"Dad," she said, "what are you doing?"

I stared at her. Wasn't quite sure what she meant. What was I doing anyway?

"Look," she said, pointing into the sink. "Why are you doing that?"

The sink was full of peelings and small white potatoes. Too many of them for the four of us.

I laughed, keeping the lid on it, making it my normal laugh. Stopping it from branching out and spreading and growing. "I must have got carried away," I said. "Daydreaming."

"What about?"

"Nothing, really."

"You sure?"

I smiled to reassure her. "Of course."

She smiled back and left.

I picked out the white skinned potatoes and put them into a pan. Scooped up the peelings and put them into the bin.

I had to try harder to keep hold of it all. Had to stay on top of it. Create the thick outer layer, the exoskeleton to keep everything in place, or my pale, fragile skin would slide and crack and the objects would spill out and the green shoots trail all down my face, and they would all know what was going on inside me.

That night after the girls had gone upstairs, I showered, performing each stage of my ablutions with great care. Wash and dry between each toe. Fold the towel evenly, matching up the two ends exactly. No overlap. No leakage. No cracking of the skin. No peeling. No white pale underbelly.

I went into my room and pulled on my pyjamas and dressing gown, did up the cord so that the two ends were exactly equal length.

I stood in front of the tanks and placed my hands together, as though in prayer, as though seeking answers.

A knock at my door. I opened it. Barbara stood there, in her work clothes.

I forced myself to smile. Forced myself to breathe. In. Out. In. Out. Forced myself to speak. "Are you off?" I asked.

"Yes. But I don't want to leave you."

"I'm absolutely fine." Smile again. Go on, just do it. Lift those corners up.

"Are you sure?"

I nodded. Move the head up and down. "Of course."

She touched my arm. I felt her hand there, felt it cold and grasping. Told myself I had a hard skin, told myself she couldn't feel what was in me. I smiled. Again.

"I'll be back in the morning," she said. "I'll see you then."

"Have a good shift," I said.

"Thanks."

She left and I heard the front door close, then her car started up and drove through the quiet village.

I sat for a while on the edge of the bed. On the edge. The very edge.

Breathe. In. Out. In. Out.

I took the lid off each tank in turn. The female watched me, seeing a multitude of me, a repeated image of me seen through her compound eye; each small, separate me adding to the one true me.

The river was full and I walked across the rough common land and stood by the bank, in the night air.

I stood on the edge of the water. On the edge of the land. The edge of the country.

The objects in my head were free-floating. My thoughts moving when I didn't want them to.

The girls were upstairs, anchored to their beds, Tilly's hand clutching the hair she had pulled from her own head, the skin raw. They were safe for the time being, but tomorrow was going to come.

It was not enough for them. I was not enough for them.

The water flowed past, pulled by the moon.

The pull of the moon.

The place at the end of the river. Where sky and sea meet and there is nothing else. Just that thin line between them.

Water, earth, sky. Bleak. Elemental.
And I thought: an act of love.
Yes.
Something safe. Simple. Pure.

Rachel

Unable to sleep, I kept turning things over in my mind. One moment telling myself I should have been firmer, he was in no state to have them, that I should just get out of bed and go and fetch them, the next moment telling myself I was being stupid, they were fine, would have a good weekend with him, and come back to me on Sunday afternoon hungry, happy to be home. And anyway Barbara would be there, to keep an eye on them.

The indecision made me feel ill at ease, but also prevented me from actually doing anything, and I stayed in bed, in a state of paralysis.

I closed my eyes, tried to think of nothing but sleep, but the unease remained.

I got out of bed and went into the bathroom, turned on the light. Pushing my hair back off my face, I looked at myself. My new self. My older self. Loosening skin, smaller eyes. Grey roots and dry, dyed hair which was too long; where I'd previously thought it softened my face and flattered me, I could now see it for what it was: dead cells and vanity.

I picked up the small scissors from the shelf, grabbed my hair and started cutting. I had to hack and saw at it, and the sound of the blades slicing through its thickness was loud and raw. I didn't stop until I held a bunch of cut hair in my hand.

I laid it on the edge of the bath, deep red, the ends faded. Then I continued, unevenly, until it was about two inches long all over my head. Ragged and rough.

The look of the hair on the white porcelain repulsed me and I put it into the bin. Then I ran the bath and got in and forced myself to lie down, until my skin was red with the heat. I dunked my head under the water and washed my hair, the shortness of it unfamiliar under my hands, my scalp stinging.

Loose hair floated on the surface and bubbles clung to my skin, in a line along the scar on my belly. I brushed them away.

The house had become too empty, too quiet, and I'd had enough of the silence. It was too loud, this kind of silence, ringing in my ears, forcing me to listen to the inner voices that came from somewhere deep down below.

I sank my head back under the scalding water, imagined it seeping in through the surface of my skin, cleansing the inside of my mind.

Tilly

Some people have one house. Some people have two.

Some people live in houses made of ice. They sleep in animal skins. And some people live in houses made of sticks. Their houses are like nests and they lie in beds of moss which are really soft.

A house looks after the people inside it. The windows are eyes and the door is a mouth. When the curtains are closed that means the eyes are shut and everyone goes to sleep.

Manty lives in a glass tank and there are no curtains. If I had a pet like Manty I would make some curtains and I would close them at night.

The window in the room at the top of Barbara's house frightened me. There were no curtains over it because it is on a slope and curtains do not like slopes. I kept thinking I would be able to see a face looking through the window, watching me. Grace told me not to be silly, that no one would be big enough to look through a window on a roof.

She didn't know that. She said that to keep me quiet.

There could have been a big eye looking in on me. Watching me.

Andrew

When I dressed myself the following morning I imagined my clothes as a hard outer shell, an exoskeleton. I locked each piece of it over my soft skin and body, and closed myself in. I needed something to get me through the day. Something to hold my inner world in, while the outer world played itself out around me.

I divided up the day by mealtimes; time to prepare, time to cook, time to clear up. Between lunch and the evening meal, Barbara got out of bed and spent the afternoon with the girls, making things from scraps of material. I stayed in the kitchen and then, when I had run out of things to do, I went outside and tidied the garden. And when I had done that I cleaned out the tanks, though the soil was clean and moist and warm. I fed the mantids their crickets and flies, and went back down to cook again.

After we'd eaten, I bathed Tilly, letting her use a whole bottle of bubble bath, and the foam spilled out on to the floor and hid her from view. Then I took her upstairs and put her to bed. Grace went to bed later, and then a bit later again, Barbara left for work. She picked up her bag and said goodbye, and once the door closed behind her, the house was filled with silence and stillness.

I breathed deeply and allowed my hard exoskeleton to ease, allowed it to break open and crack and reveal the pale softness beneath, allowed some of the interior world to spill out.

Then, just as I was about to get ready, I heard the door open again as Barbara came back in.

"I forgot my work shoes," she said, picking them up from beside the hall table. "I meant to say," she added, "maybe we could take the girls somewhere for the day tomorrow."

I couldn't speak. My soft inner skin was showing. My carapace had slipped.

"That'd be great, wouldn't it?"

I nodded, and as I moved my head up and down, the objects in my mind rolled and slipped and fell and crashed into each other, and she smiled at me and said, "I'll plan something tonight," and she left again, closing the door, and the relief was overwhelming.

I slid the bolt.

The exoskeleton cracked and raw tissue leaked out. The noise of my own breathing. Wet stain on the floor. Spillage.

But I had to tighten, focus, get the end back in sight.

I had to get ready. Do what I knew I had to do.

Three mugs of hot, sweet tea. Up to the top of the house. Under the roof, the two beds. Moon in the room through the windows and the shape of them under the covers, in the beds.

Tilly lay on her side. Raw, red skin on her scalp. Hair in one hand. Shapeless foil in the other. Eyes closed.

I have visited this upon her; I have caused all this.

I put on the bedside light. Grace on her back and her leg out and her hair over her face. I had to wake her. Carefully. Gently. Get her to rise up from the deepest of sleeps.

She stared at me, rubbing her eyes. "Is it morning?"

I had to speak to her. Needed to control the voice. Flatten it. Smooth it. "A bit early. Here, there's some tea for you."

It was time to wake Tilly. Hand on her shoulder. Showed her the tea. "Here."

The two of them sat up, rubbing eyes. Needed to normalize. Sat on Tilly's bed, picked up the mug, drank.

"What time is it?" Grace's voice, suspicious.

I concealed all vibrations, kept an even voice. "Early."

"Why have you got us up so early?"

Deep breath. Smile. "I just wanted to see you before I take you back."

"What do you mean?"

Spell out each word carefully, evenly, naturally. "I said I'd take you back early. Your mum wants you back."

Tilly pulling on my arm. "But I want to stay with you."

"I know, but I promised."

"She can't make you," Grace said.

A crack in the surface. I couldn't let them see. "She can," I said. "I have to do what she tells me to."

"Why? What can happen if you don't?" Grace asked.

Look away, or they will know what is inside me, will see it all. "She can stop me seeing you."

"How?"

"By seeing a solicitor, making a case against me. But if I do what she says, that won't happen." I had to keep the voice steady. All in the voice. "I don't want to talk about it."

Grace pushing the covers back, climbing out of bed.

Stop her, quickly. "Where are you going?"

"Just to see the time."

"It's about six."

"It looks dark."

"It's a bit cloudy." I clapped hands. Found a brisk voice, practical voice. "Come on, drink up. You too, Tilly."

"It tastes funny," Tilly said.

"It's a new make." Good, reassurance. "Drink up. That's a good girl."

"It's sweet."

I nodded. "I put extra sugar in. For a treat."

Tilly smiled. "Have I got school today?"

"No," I said. "It's Sunday." I stroked her head. Careful not to touch raw skin.

"She's doing that with her hair because she's unhappy," Grace said.

Her words shot straight into the soft flesh oozing through the gaps in the carapace.

I took another deep breath. "We're all unhappy. But we'll be all right. It's not going to go on for ever. You have to trust me."

I picked up the empty mugs and went down the stairs. Went into the kitchen. Washed the mugs. Dried them. Put everything away. Wiped the table and straightened the chairs and put the mats in a neat pile and folded the tea towel carefully. Then, I went up to my room and waited.

An act of love.

An act of sacrifice.

In the tanks, the African Devil's Flower swayed on its stick, its wings mimicking pink petals. The Kenyan mantis stood absolutely still on the earth floor, camouflaged as a dry leaf. I thought of Charles Darwin as he watched a mantid eat a gecko lizard, whole, entire; it took approximately one and a half hours.

In the top tank was the female who had eaten the exhausted male as he deposited the sperm capsule into her body. She was standing up, washing, passing her legs over her face like a cat. Meticulously cleaning herself. Licking the spines on her legs. Pulling dead fragments of him from between her knife-edge points.

I watched her until she had finished and returned to her praying position. Then I turned the switches off, one by one, and pulled out the plugs. I laid them down on the floor where, with their three pins in the air, they looked just like dead insects.

He giveth his beloved sleep.

Rachel

Another night and I still couldn't sleep. I'd wasted the day, finding ways to kill the pale hours, and then I had the dark hours of the night to get through, before they would be home.

I looked up at the bedroom ceiling, at the top of the curtains where the street light crept in.

I could hear him breathing next to me and then he turned over in bed and reached for me, ran his hand over my hair.

I took a deep breath. 'Dave,' I said. 'I made a mistake.'

'It'll grow again.'

I shook my head. Pushed his arms away. 'No. Not my hair. All this. Us.'

'Me?'

I nodded. 'Yes.'

He sat up. 'Are you going to go back to him?'

I shook my head. 'It's not that.'

'Then what?'

'All this,' I said.

'I don't understand. All what?'

'This. I need to be on my own.'

'But why? What are you going to do?'

'Nothing, just get the girls settled.'

'But Rach.'

I didn't look at him: I could hear it in his voice, the tears beginning. He tried again to hold me. I got out of bed.

'Don't do this,' he said. 'You can't do this.'

I started piling his things on to the bed. Took his bags from the wardrobe and began to fill them.

As I packed I thought perhaps I should go right over there and ask for my girls even though it was the middle of the night.

He stood in the doorway. I continued with what I was doing. I was immovable now. Invincible.

'What's happened?'

'Nothing,' I said.

'So why all this when I thought I was staying? I thought you loved me.'

'Did you?' I said. I looked at him. 'You know what I've realized? I love my children more.'

'This is because you think he has someone else.'

I closed the first bag, started filling the second. 'Of course it isn't.'

'Please. Please give me a chance.'

'No.'

He dropped to his knees beside me. 'Please.'

'Don't do that,' I said. 'It's embarrassing. Stand up.'

I walked out of the room and he followed me down to the kitchen.

'I have nowhere to go,' he said.

'You have friends. Family.'

'But I love you.'

'You don't,' I said. 'You need me. It's different.'

'No. I love you. I don't understand what's happened to make you like this.'

I picked up his watch, his lighter, his wallet. He watched as I moved around the house gathering together all his possessions, erasing every trace of him.

I carried the bags down the stairs and put them by the front door.

'Look, please just go,' I said.

'You'll change your mind.'

I shook my head. 'I won't.'

Andrew

I went round the house and gathered all the things I needed and loaded them into the boot of the car. I left the door on the latch and went upstairs, then into the attic room.

Tilly was on her side. I pulled her covers back, spread a blanket on the floor and placed her on it. I wrapped her up as I had when she was a baby, and lifted her in my arms. The weight of her in my arms, the baby weight of her, little girl weight of her. I carried her downstairs and supported her body against my leg as I opened the front door, then did the same with the back door of the car and laid her gently on the seat.

I went back into the house for Grace, who was lying flat on her back, on top of the covers. I shook her arm. I put my arms under her and went to lift her, but the weight of her was too heavy for me and I couldn't get her off the mattress. I shook her then and tried to wake her, calling her name over and over, but she wouldn't move.

A car passed by in the road outside. I thought of Tilly on the back seat. Thought of a passing car slowing and seeing her there. They would wait for me, to ask what was happening, or they might call the police, or smash the window and get her out.

I tried again to lift Grace and managed this time to get her into my arms. I half carried her, half dragged her to the doorway and turned to get through, but she was too heavy and slipped from my arms.

I had to take her out of the door and down two flights of stairs, and I couldn't even cross the room with her. I stood and thought for a while, tried to work out what to do.

It was getting lighter, getting earlier. People would be waking soon, rising. I was running out of time.

I knelt down and gathered her in my arms again, but could barely lift the dead weight of her. I half carried her back to bed and laid her on it. Tried to think of what to do.

The image came to me from deep down: the retina of my eye breaking open and clear liquid seeping out, followed by the tightly curled leaves and brightly coloured buds. I tried to stop it but couldn't. My carapace was peeling away.

I tried yet again to lift Grace, but the weight of her – oh God, the weight of her.

Time was passing. Tick tock. My head hurt. My arms were white, my arms were grubs sticking out from my exoskeleton. Soft whiteness, soft flesh. I couldn't pick her up.

And Tilly, on the back seat of the car. Someone would walk past, drive past, see her.

What to do? I could bring her back in here? But how could I do that? What would I do then when they woke? I needed to do something else.

I stood still, thinking. My arms together, my hands touching. Arms and hands like the mantid. Praying.

The one certainty, the one stillness, pureness.

And the answer came. I couldn't save Grace, but I could still save Tilly.

And so I touched Grace's hair and stroked her face, stroked her baby face, her girl face, young woman face.

Another car passed by. The world would be waking up.

An act of love.

Sacrifice.

I put a blanket over Grace and left her on the bed. I went down the stairs, closed the front door and got into the car. I started the engine and drove off.

Our bones are scattered at the grave's mouth, as when one
cutteth and cleaveth wood upon the earth.

Rachel

The door closed behind him and I could sense the silence in the house. The rightness of that silence. The aloneness of it.

I stood for a long time in the hall. I stood and thought about the time I had gone to the river at night and bathed in the cold water. The way it had felt like a vice gripping my skin. The smell of the earth and water. Water and earth.

In the living room, I looked at the lace shadows on the wall. I saw the rows of books, my father's books. I had never read them, would never read them. Andrew should have them. Not for ever, but until one of the girls wanted them.

I walked into the kitchen and took an apple from the bowl on the table. I played with it, felt the shape and weight of it in my hand, put it to my mouth, but didn't bite into the skin. Just wanted to hold it. I looked out at the garden, could see the white jasmine in the moonlight. The silhouette of the apple tree and the climbing frame.

Then, a loud banging on the front door. I knew who it

was. I heard the letterbox open and Dave calling my name. When I didn't respond, he said he would come back in the morning, that I would have changed my mind. I stayed by the window, looking out into the dark garden. He could come back over and over but I wouldn't weaken my resolve.

The silence returned to the house.

I climbed up the stairs and into Grace's room, then Tilly's. I straightened their pillows. In the morning I would come in and air their beds, tidy things up. Yes, that's what I would do. Throw open their windows. Change their sheets. Straighten their books. Get everything ready for their return.

I went up the next flight of stairs and into my room. I looked at the framed photographs of the girls hung on one wall. And then I had an odd feeling. Of what, I didn't know.

I told myself it was because of Dave leaving, and my knowledge that he would be back and I would have to remain strong to keep him away.

I told myself it was because my house was finally still, silent.

But it wasn't that either. It was something else. Something new. A deep, profound sense of unease.

Grace

The odd taste. My tongue rough like a cat's, sticking to the roof of my mouth. Dry. Coated in a layer of sand and glue.

The smell and feel of material on my face and the heat of my breath.

They weren't dreams, the scenes that had been in my head. They were too vivid for dreams. Too strong.

I pushed the fabric away, felt cool air on my face. Heard my bird, calling quietly. My eyes wouldn't open. Too busy with the pictures, plastered on the walls of my inner eyelids. I tried to move a leg, but it stayed still, heavy as wood. My foot at an angle, dead.

Was I awake or asleep? My own breathing, deep and slow. Images, shadows of what I had seen, lights trailing behind. Words scrawled out and shapes emerging from the letters and their colours and the gold and silver.

Writing on a wall? Letters. Words.

Writing, colours, right inside me.

I could hear something, but I didn't know what it was.

A banging. A door. A door with words painted all over it, the words spreading on to the walls, smeared, daubed.

My eyes, heavy as though stitched closed with thick thread. My head moved and my mouth opened again.

I was aware it was light, even with my eyes shut. I wanted to go down again, back into the place of the pictures, the heavy place, the nothing place. But the noise, and my name. Calling me, over and over. And the bird calling.

I moved my head and lifted it. So heavy on my neck. I opened my eyes, and the world was soft and blurred.

Bed, I was in bed.

Back to the heavy place. The nothing place. Let go, go down there. Slip. Slither. Drown.

Another noise. A door. This door. A voice. —Grace?

Feet coming towards me.

—Grace. What is it?

I opened my mouth to speak but couldn't. I tried to shake my head. Nothing moved.

A hand on my arm. Shaking me. —Are you ill?

—No.

Not ill. No. My voice, thick, no longer mine. My tongue swollen. Filling my mouth.

—Where is he? Where's your dad?

—I don't know. The words slurred, slow.

—He isn't here. And Tilly's gone.

My body, heavy. My blood, thick in my veins. Thick and slow.

—Grace. Grace. It's me, Barbara. What's been going on?

—I don't know.

My blood, heavy. Thick. Slow.

—Where is he? You have to tell me. Christ. Come on. He's got Tilly.

—Tilly, I echoed.

I shook my head and it was so heavy it fell to one side.

The sound of her bag unzipping, her phone dialling. And then her voice, speaking, asking for police, an ambulance.

Then the click of the phone again. —Rachel, it's me, Barbara.

Her voice, calm but scared. Far away, as if in another room, another world.

My eyes were too heavy now, the stitches pulling down, closing them.

Her phone, down. A glass of water at my lips. Talking to me, insistent, stopping my eyes from closing, forcing my brain to work. —You have to think where he could have gone, she said.

My eyes began to close again.

Barbara shook me. —You can't sleep. You're the only one who might know where he's gone.

Andrew

Tilly slept soundly on the back seat. Slept. Soundly.

Her face wrapped in the blanket, her thumb by her mouth. Her mouth slightly open. Next to her a foil animal. Silver creased head and body. Four legs and a tail. I looked out of the front windscreen, at the brown water. The mouth of the river, flowing into the sea. The sea and sky meeting. The thin line. Peace. Stillness. Ease.

But my head hurt, as though something was inside, forcing itself out, pressing against the sides of my skull, attempting to escape. The objects inside me, swelling, growing, bloating. I concentrated on my breathing, but could not slow it into the heavy rhythm I needed.

I had visited this upon them all. I had not kept each of the threads in my hand, had not woven them in the correct way, and this was the untangling. The hideous mess.

There was no other choice.

I closed my eyes and leaned back. The inside of my head was a chamber of pain, with babbling and chatter and objects rolling and pressure. My body couldn't contain it any more.

My skin would burst open and it would all come out. An eggshell crack in my skull would open wide. Let out the curls and fossils of my brain. A red slash on my belly. Intestines flowing. Spilling out, wet and slick and stinking. My grub-soft white skin would peel and split. The chaos would erupt.

I hit my head against the headrest. Had to get out. Opened the car door and stood outside, stared at the water.

Kingdom: Animal
Phylum: Arthropoda
Class: Insecta
Order: Dictyoptera
Family: Mantidae

Order – Dictyoptera.
Subgroup – Mantodea.
Families – Chaeteesidae; Metallycidae; Mantoididae; Amorphoscelidae; Eremiaphilidae; Hymenopodidae; Mantidae; Empusidae.

Praying. Preying.

I walked to the end, to the edge of the water, the littoral. Where the land meets the sea and stretches out. Out and out.

I thought of Grace, there on her bed, the dead weight of her. I couldn't save her. I thought of Tilly on the back seat. I could save her.

The sky was getting lighter. Time was running out.

★

I took Tilly's hand and uncurled her fingers, placed the foil animal inside them, then tucked the blanket back around her. I stroked her hair and listened to her breathing.

I adjusted the driver's seat as flat as it would go, then I started the engine and turned on the music and lay back and listened: the movement of the fugue passed through my body and I could feel myself sink down into the seat.

I stared up, through the sunroof, at the deep grey sky. And I waited.

Rachel

As soon as I heard the first ring I knew something must have happened. It was too early for it to be anything innocent.

I listened as Barbara spoke. Tried to stay calm. But then she asked if I had Tilly and the cold ran through my body. Each vein iced up. A metal vice round my heart.

I hung up. Grabbed my bag and keys. Ran out, slamming the door behind me. I got in the car and drove along the empty streets, through the town, over the river, towards Barbara's house.

My heart was beating too quickly and my hands were clenched on the steering wheel.

I'd felt something inside me, an inner warning, rise up when Andrew came to the house, and yet what had I done? Threatened him with a solicitor. And in the night, my deep feeling of unease, and what had I done? Stayed in bed.

I told myself he would be somewhere safe, somewhere with Tilly, he would just have taken her out. Gone on a trip, taken her as a treat. But I knew, even as I told myself this, that it was not true. It was the early hours, dawn. Where would he have gone?

I pulled up outside Barbara's house, and though I couldn't see any cars, I jumped out and rang the bell, knocked on the glass. When there was no answer I ran around to the back and looked through the double doors. The kitchen was empty.

I went back to the front of the house and stood and waited.

Grace

Barbara drove quickly, following the ambulance. Lights flashing in front of me. My body leaning on the door, my head resting against the window. The sliding of my hair on the glass. Across the land. Past the reed beds. The river, the wide mouth.

A car, his car.

She stopped and opened the car door. Ran. I watched her. She was running but I didn't know why. People in bright yellow jackets. Barbara's red jumper. Blue lights flashing.

My head, heavy.

I pushed open the door my side and got out, my legs weak, and leaned against the metal. His car door was pulled open and Dad was dragged on to the ground. Tilly lay on the ground, her eyes closed. Asleep. Asleep like me.

I closed my eyes and opened them again.

There was cardboard on his car window, something black feeding through it. Barbara lifted her head and Tilly's face was pink, and in her hand some silver.

Barbara bent down again and breathed into Tilly, like she was blowing her up.

Dad got to his knees and sat back on his heels. Rammed his fists in his eyes. Rocked.

I looked around me, and the water was brown and the sky grey instead of blue. My head was filled with clouds and I didn't know what was happening.

Then there was the sound of a police siren through the clouds and I could feel the taste in my mouth, my tongue rough like a cat's.

Could feel the green of the sky and the taste of my clouds.

The mantid played a role in the *Egyptian Book of the Dead*, as a minor deity who guided souls to heaven, continuing the commonly found myth of the mantid as giving both literal directions in the physical world, and spiritual directions in the divine world:

I have made my way into the royal palace, and it was the mantis who brought me thither.

Hail to thee, who fliest up to heaven, to give light to the stars and protect the White Crown which falleth to me.

Rachel

The walls were white gloss, yellowing, slightly grubby.
Rows of blue chairs and a machine at the end. I fed change
in, coin by coin, pressed the buttons. A thin plastic cup
dropped down and settled at the bottom of the chute. Hot
water spurted out and filled the cup.

I picked it up, holding it by the rim as the plastic was
hot and burned my hand. I carried it to the seat and sat
down, put the cup on the floor to cool. I rested my head
on my legs. Bent right forward.

What to do? How to contain this and remain there? But
there was no alternative. I sat and waited to be called back
into the room. My hand shook as I lifted the coffee to my
lips.

The doors opened and I looked up, expecting the doctor
in her white coat, but it was Barbara.

We stayed like that for a while, me holding my coffee,
Barbara by the door, waiting. Eventually she spoke. 'Can I
come and sit there?'

I nodded, and she came to sit in the chair next to mine.

'Rachel,' she said. 'I'm so sorry.'

I finished my coffee and stood to throw the cup in the bin. Sat back down.

'What can I do?' she asked.

I shook my head. 'Nothing.'

'Have you seen Grace?'

'Yes,' I said. 'I just came out while they do some tests.'

The coffee machine made a gurgling noise, as though reheating water. A woman opened the door and peered at us, then looked around and left.

'How did you find them?' I asked.

'I managed to get it out of Grace. He's been going there a lot. I didn't know.' I waited, and she hesitated, then continued. 'I didn't know the state he was in. I mean the true state. We'd planned to do something, take the girls somewhere today. I had no idea he would do something like this.'

I stared out of the window at the courtyard garden, the rectangular pond and the bench. A bird flew across the courtyard, then up the side of the building until it reached the sky and disappeared.

'Rachel,' she said.

I turned round.

'Will they be all right?'

I hesitated, looked out of the window again, then back to her. 'I don't know.'

The only sound was the occasional rumble from the coffee machine, and a distant siren that got louder as it approached, then stopped. Then the door opened and the doctor appeared in her white coat, clipboard in hand, and asked me to accompany her. As I stood up, Barbara took my hand and squeezed it.

I followed the doctor back to the room. Grace lay curled up on her side, her back to me. I walked around the bed and looked at her face, her closed eyes.

I pushed the hair away from her forehead and stroked her cheek.

She opened her eyes. 'Mum.'

I took her hand. 'I'm here.'

'Where's Tilly?'

'Lie still,' I said. 'You need to sleep.'

She struggled, as if trying to sit up. 'Where is she? I need to see her.'

'You need to sleep first.'

'I can't. Mum.'

I looked at the woman in the white coat. She nodded and we pulled the blanket and sheet back, and helped Grace to her feet.

Grace

My head had been painted white inside. It was as though my mind was newly made. There were just a few things in there. The white of the clouds. And the ambulance. Dad on the ground.

And Tilly, her pink skin and the foil animal crushed in her hand.

The two women, Mum and the woman in her white coat, put their arms under mine and guided me along the corridor.

The bed was the nearest to the nurses and it was hard to see her at first, she was so buried beneath machinery and tubes. They sat me down on one of the chairs.

Tilly's eyes were closed and her arms were resting on the sheets. The room was full of electronic noise, the machines pulsing with steady rhythms and high sounds.

Mum took one of Tilly's hands and held it. I opened my mouth to speak, my heart going too fast and my breathing shallow. The words, when they eventually came,

sounded unfamiliar, and my voice wasn't quite my own. —
What did they say?

Mum looked at me, seeming like someone else with her
short hair. —They don't know yet. They're going to do
some tests but they won't know for a bit.

She reached for my hand, so she was holding Tilly's
hand and mine.

—She's smaller, so it will have affected her more. We
just have to hope she'll be all right.

—And Dad? I asked. —How is he?

—He's fine, they've put him in a room on his own.
They've medicated him so he can get some sleep and rest.

I nodded.

We sat there for a long time, then a nurse brought us
some tea and we drank that. Mum put her cup down.

—How do you feel? she asked me.

—I'm okay, I said. Then, —Why didn't he take me
with him?

She looked up at me, our eyes meeting. —I don't know.

—What would've happened if Barbara hadn't come
home?

—We won't talk about that now, let's just see how Tilly
is.

—And what if he'd gone somewhere else?

—We're not talking about it now. You have to get well
first.

We sat and listened to the machines. Then I looked up
at Mum.

—Mum, I said. —I still want to see him.

The mantid has the *hypognathous*, the inverted triangular head, and both simple and compound eyes. The simple eyes are three ocelli, also in a triangular pattern and situated between the antennae. The two compound eyes have up to 10,000 ommatidia each.

The mantid has two raptorial front legs which have been developed to seize prey, the femur and tibia having rows of sharp spines. The front legs are clasped together as though in 'prayer', and the mantid combines a highly developed method of attack with extraordinary patience and camouflage skills, making it a ruthless and brilliant survivor.

'The mantis is not strong enough to stop the bullock cart, but is brave enough to try.'

Andrew

Some time has passed. A week: perhaps less, perhaps slightly more; I have found it difficult to keep track of the passing days.

I think it's around 5.00 a.m., and I can hear the rain outside, the first rain for weeks. I adjust the pillow behind my head and lie back, my eyes fixed on the ceiling.

I am being given medication that should dull and tarnish my mind. It's designed to conceal past events from me. It fails. Fragments of knowledge exist inside me and I am able to piece them together until, like the marks on newsprint, the various images create a whole understanding.

They are small objects in my mind, these snippets of knowledge. They are not as clear as they should be, and they are not wholly anchored, but they do not roll with such wild abandon.

Things I know:

I know I took her in the car with me.

I know I left the older girl there, on the bed to sleep.

I recall the smell as it entered the car. And the door

being wrenched open. And the young girl with the oxygen mask.

I know what I did. But it was the only thing to do.

I will have to see them. Talk to them.

How?

They do not call this the psychiatric unit, but I know that is what it is. I am encouraged to get out of my bed and walk into another room where a television plays and people sit at tables with packs of cards, moving them and sorting them.

I wait. I wait for the time when they decide they have to sit me down and begin to discuss what has happened.

Yesterday I had a visitor. I woke to find him on the chair beside me. It took a while to register his identity, but eventually my brain searched through the medicated layers and found an answer. The sun came in and illuminated his pale hair, revealing strands of red. I waited for him to say something but he didn't. He sat in silence.

After he had gone I found the stack of books he'd left behind for me. I picked up the top one and stroked the cover, then opened it at random.

Throughout history, we see the mantid appear in folklore and mythology. This is perhaps because of its distinctive posture, but also because of its cannibalistic nature, and highly developed and deeply instinctive survival skills.

I closed the book and held it close to me.

★

It is afternoon, I think, and the light has filled the room.

I think of getting out of bed and walking into the other room. I go to swing my legs out of the bed, but before I do, I see that someone is standing in the doorway of my room.

The sun is behind her and I do not make out every feature on her face at first, but I know who it is.

I turn my face away.

But she does not go. Instead she comes into the room and approaches me. She pulls a chair up to my bed and sits down. I keep my face tight to the wall.

She takes my hand in hers.

My hand is pale and white and oh so tender in her hand, and I can say nothing. I can say nothing.

She holds me. She holds me.

I feel myself get lost, the white softness of me in the white sheets, and I feel her holding my hand and my mind escapes into the few certainties that exist.

The mantid's eye, the compound eye, is made up of the ommatidia, the visual receptors. Each ommatidium consists of the lens, a crystalline cone, visual cells, pigment cells. As objects move across the eyes, the ommatidia are switched on and off, giving a flicker effect. The composite of the responses of the ommatidia creates a mosaic image, and the quality of that image is dependent upon the number of ommatidia; the more images, the clearer the overall picture.

Rachel

Back at home, I stand at the window and look out over the trees. I can see the first change in the colour of the chestnut leaves; the edges are beginning to curl and go orange.

The television is on behind me, its dull, constant voice a welcome distraction, something to fill my head and push thoughts away. That's the idea, anyway, but of course it doesn't work. The thoughts creep through breaks in the sound, find their way in.

And I stand here and look at the trees, smell the new, fresh, rain-sodden air.

And while I stand here, Grace is in her room below mine. I imagine her in bed, curled up on her side, in the deep place of sleep.

And while I stand here, Tilly is still in that hard, high bed, which we will visit later today. We will sit there for a long time and take her hands in ours and talk to her, and Grace will read to her from her book, the story of the mantid and the girl with the red dress. Then I will stay there while Grace leaves and goes to her father's room, as she does every day, where she will sit with him.

And I will go there and sit with him, but not yet.

I can't. Not yet.

I stand at the window and look out over the trees. I run my hand through my hair and am shocked again by the shortness of it. The new feel of it.

I try not to blame myself, but it is not easy. It is not my fault, I tell myself, I could not have foreseen this. And yet. And yet.

The small, thin voice creeps around in my mind, whining its questions, asking what I contributed, how I might have prevented it from happening. That is why I walk to the television and turn the volume up, to drown out this voice inside me, except that the louder I turn it, the louder the inner voice becomes.

The days stretch ahead, day after day after day. Waiting for news, waiting for results, waiting to see if there will be lasting damage, waiting as Tilly's body fights to recover and return to normality.

And I know that one day, when he too has recovered, we will have to sit down and talk about what happened, about what nearly happened.

And one thing I want to do. Will do today. I will go to Barbara's house and thank her properly, and I will go into Andrew's room and throw the dead insects away, and clean and disinfect the tanks. Prepare them for the day he replaces the mantids.

But now, right now, standing here, I think of Grace in the room below, the two of us in this house where there were once four.

And suddenly, overwhelmingly, I want to go and see her.

I want to push open her door and enter her room. I want to wake her and tell her to move up so I can sit down, just the two of us in the room. I want to touch her. Talk to her.

I walk across the room and turn the door handle. I walk out of my room, and down the stairs.

Grace

I am in bed, awake. Unable to sleep. Rain falls outside the window, and I can hear the television from upstairs, from Mum's room.

My bird is in her cage, which sits by the window. Occasionally she makes sounds at me, and I make them back. Right now, as I watch her, she tips her head to the side, and settles into sleep. Her wings are covered in feathers, and she likes to stretch them, practising. I am starting to let her out, and when she smells the fresh air, her wings begin to flex and I know it won't be long now before she can lift herself up into the sky.

I am in bed, awake. But it is not my bird who keeps me awake. It's what's inside my head. Sounds and images play over and over, forcing me to try to put them in order, to make sense of them.

The white of the clouds against the grey sky, the gold of the letters, the curve of the words.

In the house with the red bricks and slate roof, high up on the river bank, the words on the walls: *The words of the*

Lord are pure words: as silver tried in a furnace of earth, purified seven times. I thought I had found something. I thought I had an answer. But I am beginning to see there are no answers, there are only questions.

There are only things that happen. Some people see a pattern. Some don't.

These days have a pattern. I rise, eat, then we go to the hospital.

We sit, one on either side of her bed, and I read. I read the story of the mantis and the girl. She can hear me. She will be listening, taking it in, and it will be sinking right down inside her, making sense and shape.

And then, when I have read the book, I leave her side and I walk the corridors, and I do what I have done every day: I sit by Dad's bed, while he slips in and out of dreams, still unaware of what happened, what he tried to do.

I am in bed, awake. Unable to sleep. Rain falls outside the window, and I can hear the television from upstairs, from Mum's room.

The house is so empty. Just the two of us, where there were once four.

I ache. I hurt for what we had.

But then I hear the silence as the television is switched off. A door opens.

I can hear feet on the stairs.

I lie and listen and the feet stop outside my door. I hear

the knock of her knuckles on the wood, I see the handle turn, watch as her face appears.

Mum comes in and stands by my bed. She touches my legs and I move them so she has room to sit down. She takes my hand in hers and holds it.

Then I lean forward and pull her towards me and she lies on the bed with me and we hold each other, as we have not done for years.

Tilly

I am in a tank. I have a red dress on and my arms are raised up.

There is a face staring at me through the glass. Two huge eyes. They have black dots in them and they look at me.

My bed moves. It is soft and hard. It is high and low.

I know who I am.

I am a girl in a red dress in a tank.

I have a sister. I have a mother. I have a father. He has strong arms and can hold me in them, can carry me.

My throat is sore. I have a sore throat.

I hear a voice talking to me. A voice telling me a story.

Manty the baby praying mantis was born in a glass tank in a room in a house.

Manty holds me with her arms and she tips her triangle head to the side and she smiles at me. We have a bed inside the tank. It is made of sticks that are in a circle. It is a nest and it is lined with moss. I lie in the moss because my legs are soft. I can't stand up because my legs are soft.

I am in a tank. The eyes stare in at me. The black dots are in the middle of the blue.

Then the eyes move and I can see out of the glass.

I try to stand up in my nest of sticks and this time my legs are harder. I stand up and I get out of my nest and I walk across the earth. I stand in front of the glass side of the tank and I try to climb. But my legs slip down and there is nothing to hold on to. I try again but I slip down again and fall.

I lie on the earth, but I will try again. I know if I keep trying enough times, one day I will be able to do it. I will be able to climb right up the side of the tank and push open the lid, and I will come out. I will.